· AN USBORNE

DESIGN & DECORATE YOUR ROOM

Felicity Everett and Paula Woods

Interior design consultant: Jill Blake
Edited by Janet Cook
Designed by Nerissa Davies

Illustrated by Jackie Marks and Nick Williams
Additional illustrations by Frances Castle, Nicky Dupays
and Paul Sullivan

Commissioned photography by Keith Parry

Interior design careers consultant: Helen Giles
Additional designs by Jane Felstead
Stencils designed by John Pye

C ontents

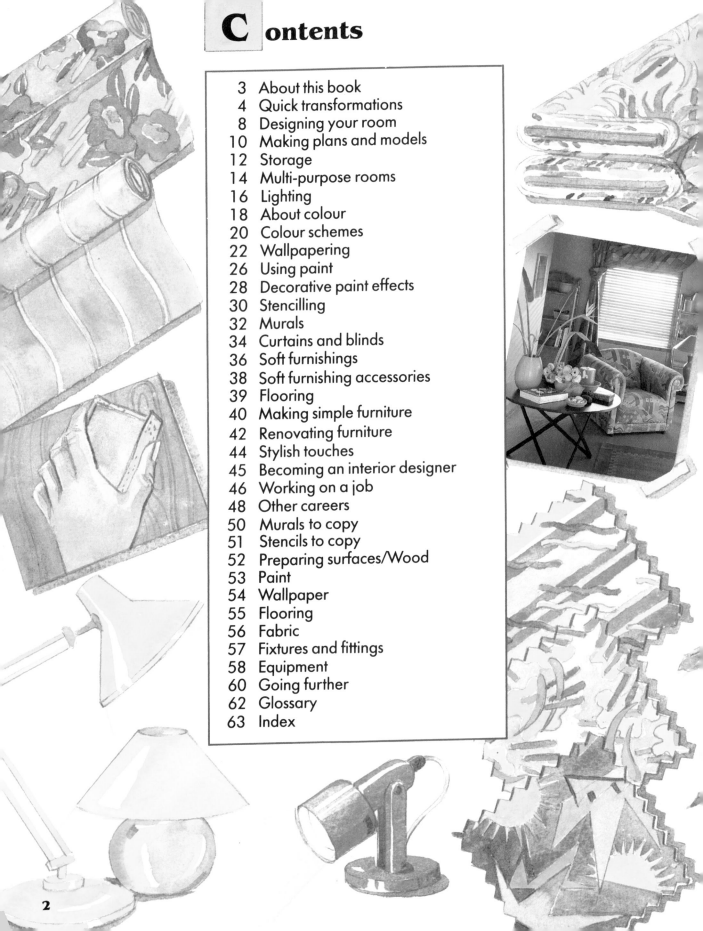

About this book

Most people have thought about, even had a go at, decorating their room. But designing it first – isn't that complicated and expensive? Don't you need professional help? Not necessarily.

This book explains why design is the natural partner to decoration. When you choose a particular colour of paint, hang a poster, or rearrange the furniture, you are making decisions about design. Pages 8-21 show you how to order these decisions and choose priorities. Covering all aspects of design from storage to lighting and colour schemes, it also shows you how to make plans and models to help you visualize your design. The more limited the possibilities seem, whether it is because your room is small, or shared, or because you don't have much money to spend, the more worthwhile it is thinking through the problems first.

Once you have a design you are happy with, the next stage is decorating. You can find out all about the practical side of painting, wallpapering and making curtains and soft furnishings on pages 22-38. Clear, step-by-step instructions show what to do and there are lots of practical tips to help you get a really professional finish.

If designing your own room whets your appetite for more, you can find out about the world of professional interior design on pages 45-49. There is a down-to-earth look at what the job really entails, covering the hard work and mundane aspects, as well as the more glamorous side. There is a glimpse behind the scenes of a typical job, and, if you want to go even further, a list of books and interior design courses.

Technical terms

Technical terms crop up in both the theoretical and practical aspects of interior design. In this book, these have either been explained, or everyday words used in their place. However, useful terms which you will meet often, have been printed in **bold italics** wherever they first appear in a section, and are explained in the glossary on page 62.

Quick transformations

If your accommodation is temporary or if you like your room to reflect the latest trend, it is not a good idea to spend a lot of money on a permanent change of *décor*. A quick, economical revamp would probably be a better solution.

Walls

Fabric is good for covering walls temporarily as it can be re-used when you move. Furnishing fabric is very expensive for covering large areas, but used sparingly, and with unusual trimmings (such as those in the photograph on the left), it can give your room a sumptuous feel. For larger areas you could buy plain white *sheeting* and dye it, or decorate it using fabric paints. Stretch it taut over your walls, or drape it softly, and secure it with tacks or staples (you will need a staple gun).

Paper is a good alternative to fabric, although it is less hardwearing. Try using the kind which professional photographers use for backdrops. You can buy it from photographic suppliers – it comes in wide rolls and lots of different colours.

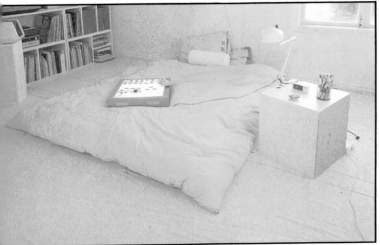

Floors

The quickest and cheapest way to cover an unsightly carpet is with a large, inexpensive rug. Fabric is not generally suitable as a floor covering. However, if you don't mind banning outdoor shoes from the room, hessian, thick canvas or window dresser's felt* are all good, relatively cheap alternatives to conventional flooring.

Hessian or canvas can be stencilled or can be decorated free-hand with fabric paints. Window dresser's felt comes in a wide range of bright colours, so looks good left plain (see left). Make sure you tack each length down securely to avoid accidents.

Ceilings

An eye-catching way to cover your ceiling is to drape fabric from a central point, creating a tent effect, as in the picture on the left. This works best if the ceiling is fairly high. Measure the distance from the centre of the ceiling to the corner of your room and add on a few centimetres for the hem. This is the width your fabric will need to be (you could join lengths together if necessary). Now measure the distance around the walls and add on half to twice the same amount for gathering. This is the length your fabric will need to be.

Stitch along the *selvedge* of the fabric with large tacking stitches, using heavy-duty thread. Leave a long thread end when you have finished. Repeat about 5cm in from the first line of stitching. Gather up the fabric by pulling on the two thread ends. Ask a friend to help you fix the fabric to the ceiling. Position the gathered part at the centre and staple or tack it in place. Where the edges of the fabric meet the corners of the room, turn the edges under and staple, or tack them in position.

You could also make a decorative fabric rosette as a centre-piece

* You can buy this from a shop fitter's.

Windows

To enhance a good view, or an attractive window, without going to the trouble of making curtains, you could drape fabric over a curtain pole or flexible curtain track. If privacy is important, you will need a blind or net curtain as well, as these window dressings cannot be pulled across the window without spoiling the arrangement.

Although they look lavish, most of the effects shown on the right take less fabric than real curtains would, as they only use one width of fabric, rather than the one and a half to two and a half widths it takes to make normal curtains. Draping the fabric so that it hangs attractively takes a bit of practice, but is well worth the effort.

Furniture

If you want to give a new look to old or tatty furniture, particularly upholstered items, such as armchairs and sofas, all you need is a piece of furnishing fabric, or a cheap cotton bedspread which is large enough to cover the item completely, with fabric to spare. Throw it over the item of furniture and tuck it down the sides as firmly as possible. If you find that the fabric won't stay in place, secure it with safety pins or tack it neatly, making sure that the pins or stitches will not show.

Smaller soft furnishings, such as cushion covers and table cloths make a room cosy and can easily be improvised using remnants of furnishing fabric. To save time, trim the edges of the fabric with *pinking shears,* instead of hemming them.

This old screen has been renovated by attaching new pieces of fabric to each panel.

String knotted around an improvised cushion makes a witty finishing touch.

A cheap bedspread thrown over this dated armchair gives it a contemporary feel.

This floor-length cloth conceals a battered old table.

Beds

If you live in one room, there is always the problem of what to do with your bed during the day.

One solution is to transform it into a seating area, another is to have a *Futon*, or a bed that folds up into the wall. Alternatively, if you have the space, you could turn your bed into a decorative feature, by draping it with fabric or screening it off, like a four-poster.

The effects you can achieve vary from extravagant-looking swags, to a simple, minimalist look. The ideas on the right can all be achieved easily and cheaply.

Here, a shortened curtain pole mounted at right angles to the wall supports a simple canopy, made from a single length of fabric.

Small hooks, screwed into the ceiling support the fine threads from which this muslin canopy is suspended. This method is only suitable for light fabrics.

Curtain poles at the head and foot of this bed are suspended from the ceiling on wires. A length of fabric draped over the top completes the dramatic effect.

Here a coronet (semi-circular bracket) is fixed to the wall to provide support for the two curtains. *Tie-backs* keep the curtains out of the way.

Shower curtains, hung on curtain tracks supported from the walls create an unusual effect. They also provide privacy when required.

Lighting

Lighting can create astonishing optical illusions. If you have the sockets available, buying one or two carefully chosen lamps can be the simplest way of transforming your room. If you don't have much money to spare, there are some even cheaper ideas on the right.

When entertaining, use lights to highlight decorative objects, such as this plant.

For a quick change of mood, try replacing the light bulbs in all your lamps and light fittings with coloured ones.

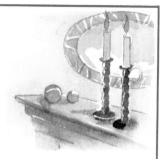

Candles create a romantic effect for a special occasion. Keep them away from anything flammable*.

Never leave candles burning when you leave a room.

Instant storage

When you are planning a room from scratch, finding permanent places to put things is one of the first things you should do. However, sometimes going back to basics just isn't practical and you have no choice but to improvise. Below are some ideas for quick, cheap, short-term storage.

Tea chests can make useful containers* for things which you don't ▶ often use. Pile up the contents and place the tea chest over the top, open side down. Disguise it with a a piece of fabric.

Plastic, stackable storage racks cost very little and can ▶ be used for all kinds of things, from hobby equipment to shoes. If they cannot be kept out of sight, buy storage racks in a colour which matches your *décor* and keep them tidy enough to display.

◀ A large wicker basket can be a good place to store things like jumpers and scarves, which will not suffer from being folded. Keep the basket away from direct sunlight, or your things will fade.

Some planks of wood and a pile of ▶ bricks are all you need to make simple instant shelves.
Stack the planks on the bricks, as shown, taking care to keep the bricks positioned directly above one another. To prevent long shelves from bowing in the middle, build a central brick support.

If you lack hanging space, you could ◀ store coats and hats or even indoor garments on a coat-stand. You can sometimes find these in junk shops. Restore them using techniques such as those on pages 42-43.

Creating atmosphere

Many different things contribute to the atmosphere in your room. Obvious things like its colour and style play a large part, but there are many small things which make an enormous difference to how pleasant it is to be in.

★ Pot pourri in a bowl or basket looks pretty and makes your room smell good. For an eastern flavour, try burning joss sticks.

★ Play tapes or records which match the mood you want to create. For example, background music for a dinner party; soothing music for relaxing; dance music for a party, and so on.

★ If you are entertaining, arrange the seats so your guests can talk to each other easily.

★ Fresh or dried flowers look bright and welcoming. Choose colours which complement your colour scheme.

★ Don't worry if your room looks lived-in. A very tidy room can be impersonal and off-putting. Books, magazines and evidence of hobbies add interest to your room.

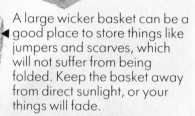

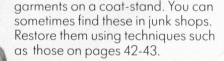

* First hammer down any tacks and remove rough metal banding.

7

Designing your room

The principles of good design are the same, whether you have a pittance or a fortune to spend. On the next four pages you can find out how to analyse your needs, match them up to practical design ideas and then try them out in sketches and plans.

Write yourself a brief

Professional interior designers work to a brief. This means that they ask their client all about their needs and preferences. A brief can help you to be practical about the way you design your own room. Ask yourself the following questions and jot down the answers.

★ **What kind of person are you?**

A good design will suit your lifestyle. For example, if you are a hoarder, there is no point striving for a spartan, *hi-tech* look, as you won't have anywhere to put anything.

★ **Do you get bored with your surroundings easily?**

If you like changing your furniture around and trying out different looks, you will need a flexible room design. Try not to fall for fashion fads which will look dated and need replacing in a short time.

★ **Do you share with anyone else or use your room for more than one purpose?**

If you have a room mate, discuss your plans together. If you disagree about the design, there are ways to divide the room into separate areas and harmonize different styles of *décor* (see page 14). You can use the same ideas even if your room isn't shared.

Your room

The shape, size, proportions and architectural style of your room define the area within which you, as its designer, have to work. On the right you can see a small room, designed to utilise fully the available space and enhance the room's rustic architectural style.

Size and shape

The size and shape of your room will determine the amount of furniture you can fit in, and the space available for different activities. Here, the alcoves provide storage for clothes and books, as well as a study area. The chest of drawers under the window doubles as storage space and additional seating. A bolster and scatter cushions convert the bed into a comfortable sofa.

The ceiling is low and the room rather angular, so a pale colour scheme has been chosen to make walls and ceiling recede, while draped curtains soften the harsh lines of the window wall and an oval rug gives variety of shape and breaks up the floor area.

Making a budget

Calculate how much money you have and divide it up sensibly. Jot down some alternative ways of achieving the finished effect you would like, then estimate how much each plan would cost and choose the one which is within your price range, for example:

Room needs: shelving, new colour scheme, new soft furnishings, bed which converts into seating area. Plans A and B on the right show alternative solutions, with the most expensive items at the top, and the cheapest at the bottom of the lists.

Plan A
Buy Futon
Buy wallpaper & border
Buy materials to make shelves
Dye curtains & duvet cover
Buy remnants of fabric for cushions

Structure

On a limited budget, major structural changes are not really feasible. However, you should consider the effect which even superficial changes will have on neighbours and other people in the building.

Here, for example, the stripped and varnished floorboards enhance the natural look of the room, but without the sound-proofing properties of carpet above, the noise level in the room below will be increased.

Style

Many modern rooms are featureless, which gives you the freedom to decorate them in any style you like. A period room, such as this one, however, often has a distinctive architectural style. Here the cottagey effect of the sloping walls, latticed window and old-fashioned fireplace are echoed in the traditional designs of the rug and fabrics, and the natural textures of bare wood, wicker and dried flowers.

If your room has a period flavour which doesn't appeal to you, choose a contrasting style of *décor* which will harmonize, rather than clash with it.

Focal points

Some rooms have a natural focal point (a place to which your attention is automatically drawn). Here, the fireplace makes a cosy centre piece in winter and an attractive one, decorated with dried flowers, in summer.

If your room lacks an obvious focal point, you could create one. A lavish bed canopy (see page 6), a trompe l'oeil mural (see page 33) or a well-displayed collection of decorative objects are all good ideas.

Plan B
Buy curtain fabric & new duvet cover
Buy self-assembly shelving units
Buy paint for walls
Make cushions to go on bed

The design process

Below is a flow chart showing the different planning stages involved in designing your room.

1. Write yourself a brief (see opposite page).

2. Look at the shape, size, style and structure of your room and decide whether it has any obvious focal points. Think about ways of enhancing its good points and overcoming its bad ones.

3. Do some research to find inspiration for a suitable style of *décor*. Look at books, magazines, museums and art galleries. Think about the decorative styles you have seen in stately homes, on foreign holidays and at friends' houses. Jot down your ideas and collect pictures of rooms and objects which inspire you.

4. Make quick sketches of different design ideas. Work out a budget for each one, to help you to decide which options are within your means.

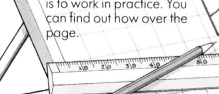

5. When you have come up with a suitable design, it is useful to draw a scale plan, or even make a model to see how likely it is to work in practice. You can find out how over the page.

Making plans and models

Once you have a rough idea of the style of room you would like, and the different purposes you want it to serve, it is a good idea to make a detailed plan or model. A two-dimensional (2-D) floor plan will help you to decide on the layout of the room, without humping heavy furniture around. A three-dimensional (3-D) model has the added advantage that you can judge heights, try out colour schemes and lighting effects.

Making a 2-dimensional plan

First, measure the length and breadth of your room and any deviations in its shape, such as bay windows and alcoves. Note the length and width of your fittings and furniture.

Equipment checklist

- Graph paper
- Ruler
- HB pencil
- Rubber
- Scissors
- Retractable rule (for measuring room)
- Coloured marker
- Glue

1. Decide on a scale for your plan. A suitable one might be 1m room space to 25cm graph paper. Carefully draw the room to scale on the graph paper, as shown.

2. Mark any permanent fixtures such as radiators, sockets and so on. Moveable items will have to be planned around these.

3. On a new sheet of graph paper, draw the shapes of your furniture to the same scale as the room plan. Colour them in, and try them in various places on your plan.

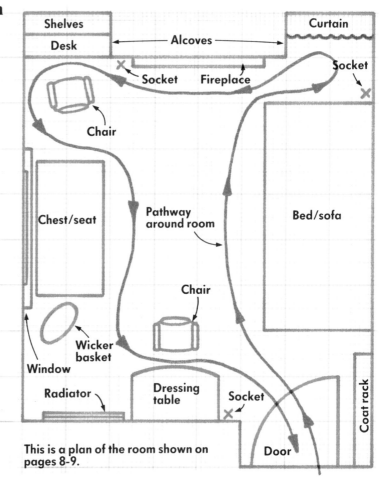

This is a plan of the room shown on pages 8-9.

Labels in plan: Shelves, Desk, Alcoves, Curtain, Socket, Fireplace, Socket, Chair, Chest/seat, Pathway around room, Bed/sofa, Chair, Wicker basket, Window, Radiator, Dressing table, Socket, Coat rack, Door

Practical planning

Sockets and switches. Use your plan to check that these are accessible, and that you have power points where you need them. Extension leads and adaptors can give you more flexibility, but do not overload sockets or allow wires to trail across your path. You can find out more about lighting design on pages 16-17.

Furniture. Always allow for *dado rails*, skirting boards and so on. These might prevent an item of furniture from fitting into its alloted space.

Allow for drawers and doors to open; leave room to stretch your legs in front of a sofa; make sure you can fit people, as well as dining chairs around your table, and so on.

Pathways. Draw dotted lines on your plan to indicate the possible routes you may take around the room. If you find that a particular arrangement of furniture wastes space or prevents you from gaining access to areas which you use frequently, redesign the layout until you have a more convenient arrangement.

Maximizing space. Inventive storage solutions and versatile furniture can make a big difference to a cramped room. If your room has a high ceiling, consider building a bed platform (see page 13), or floor-to-ceiling shelving or cupboards. It is best to try this out on a 3-D model first, to check that you get the dimensions right.

Making a 3-dimensional model

Before you start, measure all the dimensions of your room and furniture and note the exact positions of doors and windows. Work out a suitable scale for your model*.

Equipment checklist

- Flexible white card
- Clear sticky tape

- Graph paper
- Steel ruler and scalpel
- Pencil
- Cutting mat or thick card
- Scissors

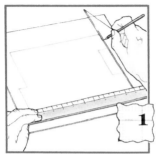
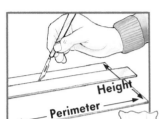
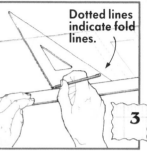
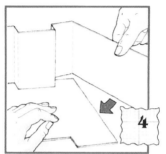

Height

Perimeter

Dotted lines indicate fold lines.

1. Draw a scale floor plan on white card (see opposite). Cut it out then measure its **perimeter**. Note the length of each wall and the depth of each recess in turn. Add the measurements together, to find the total wall length.

2. Now scale down the height of your room and make a note of the scaled-down measurement. Draw a rectangle on your white card, the length of the perimeter times the scaled-down height. Cut it out.

3. Use your perimeter measurements to plot the places where your card will fold to make the corners of the room. Mark them and the hinged side of the door with dotted lines. Mark the door and windows with solid lines.

4. Using a scalpel and steel ruler, cut carefully along the solid lines and score, then fold, along the dotted ones. Fit the walls carefully around the floor plan and use small pieces of clear sticky tape to fix them in place.

Using the model to design your room

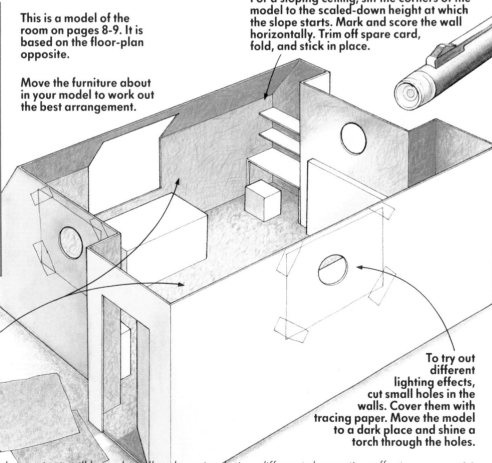

Modelling furniture

It is best to simplify your model furniture. Basic rectangles and squares can stand for beds, chests, tables etc.

The models must be to the same scale as the room model. Write down the scaled-down measurements of each piece of furniture, in order, as in step 2 above. Draw them on card, then make up, as for the room model.

This is a model of the room on pages 8-9. It is based on the floor-plan opposite.

Move the furniture about in your model to work out the best arrangement.

For a sloping ceiling, slit the corners of the model to the scaled-down height at which the slope starts. Mark and score the wall horizontally. Trim off spare card, fold, and stick in place.

To try out colour schemes, stick tissue paper over the walls and floor. You could also use real samples of fabric, carpet etc, but remember that any pattern will look deceptively large on your model.

To try out different lighting effects, cut small holes in the walls. Cover them with tracing paper. Move the model to a dark place and shine a torch through the holes.

* The bigger your model, the easier it will be to handle when simulating different decorating effects.

S torage

Creating a good storage system for all your personal belongings is vital. Even the most beautifully decorated room can be ruined by a lot of clutter. Below there are lots of ideas of ways to use a limited amount of space as effectively as possible.

Planning your storage

When working out where to store something, ask yourself the following questions;

1. How accessible does it need to be? You should be able to reach everyday items without standing on tiptoe or bending down. For example, suitcases could be stored high up or low down, whereas clothes and cosmetics are best stored between waist and shoulder height.

2. Do you want to display it , or hide it away? You can make a feature of attractive items, such as books, jewellery or brightly coloured files. However, remember that too much clutter can make a small room look even smaller.

3. Is it something you only use or wear in the summer or winter? A winter coat, for example, will be no use in the summer and will take up valuable wardrobe space. Instead, store out-of-season items elsewhere until you need them.

Practical tips

Don't skimp on hanging space. You will find it difficult to take out and put away clothes that are packed too closely together.

Hang shirts up, rather than folding them in drawers; they are easier to get to, and won't need ironing again before you can wear them.

Storage ideas

A brand new built-in storage system can be very effective, but may prove too much for your budget. Don't despair; there are masses of ways you can improvise without spending a fortune. Here are a few ideas;

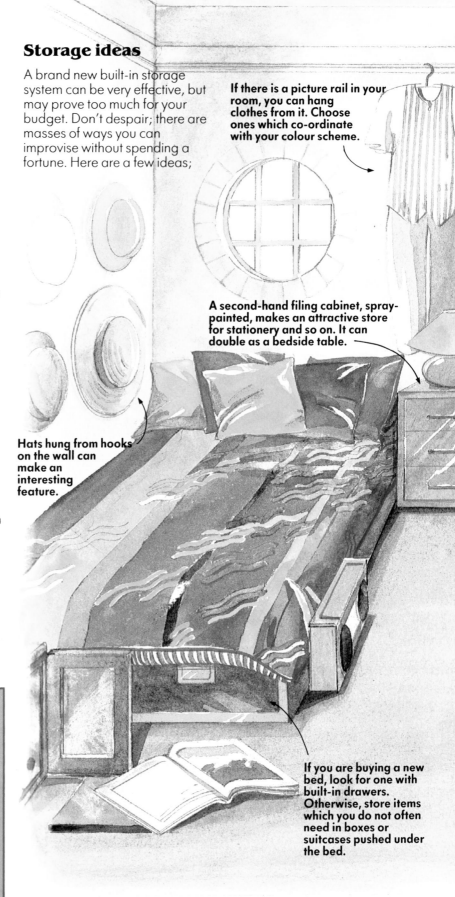

If there is a picture rail in your room, you can hang clothes from it. Choose ones which co-ordinate with your colour scheme.

A second-hand filing cabinet, spray-painted, makes an attractive store for stationery and so on. It can double as a bedside table.

Hats hung from hooks on the wall can make an interesting feature.

If you are buying a new bed, look for one with built-in drawers. Otherwise, store items which you do not often need in boxes or suitcases pushed under the bed.

A pole fixed between two surfaces makes a good rack from which to hang extra clothes. You can hide it with a curtain.

Blinds can be used to hide messy shelves.

Cardboard boxes can be filled, labelled and kept out of sight.

Wire baskets are good for storing odds and ends, as you can spot what you need instantly.

Wire mesh, mounted on the wall, stores jewellery and makes an interesting feature.

A blanket box can store bulky jumpers, and doubles as extra seating.

If you keep shoes in their boxes, you can stack them on top of each other. It is a good idea to label them clearly.

Putting up shelves

Shelves make extremely useful and efficient storage. There are a lot of different sorts you can buy in kit form, and most can be put up without much trouble. It is also fairly easy to make your own from planks of wood and bought brackets.

When deciding on the sort to buy, you should take into consideration what you are planning to put on them. A hi-fi, for example, will need stronger shelves than those used to display ornaments. Work out how deep they need to be in advance; many large stores will cut your shelving to size.

On the right you can see the main sorts of supports available. The first two systems are attached to the face of an open wall. The rest are attached to two side walls. See page 57 for to mount shelves.

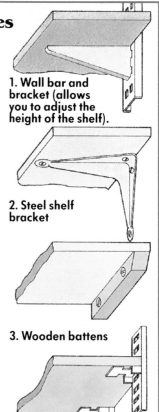

1. Wall bar and bracket (allows you to adjust the height of the shelf).

2. Steel shelf bracket

3. Wooden battens

4. Track and clip supports (for light loads only).

5. Plastic peg supports (very light loads only).

Beds

A bed takes up a lot of space, but this can be used to your advantage. By putting it on a platform, you can put storage units or shelves underneath it. Alternatively, you could opt for a split-level solution, with your bed raised high above the floor. The space beneath it can then be used as a seating or working area.

Multi-purpose rooms

Few people have the luxury of only needing to use their bedroom to sleep in. More often than not, it has to double up as a study, a sitting room, a dining room, or all three. If you play a musical instrument or belong to a band, you may also need to use it as a place to practise.

On these pages, there is advice on how to create separate areas within your room and how to make it serve all the purposes you have in mind. You can also find out how best to avoid squabbles over territory when sharing your room with a brother or sister, or a friend.

Using colour

You can use colour as a way of identifying separate areas in your room. It is important to consider mood when deciding which colours will suit an area best.

In a study-bedroom, for example, relaxing colours such as peach, beige and cream might be suitable for the bedroom area. Stronger, more stimulating tones, such as orange and terracotta would be better for the study area.

Dividing the room up

Furniture such as cupboards and drawers can be placed at right angles to a wall to make a semi-permanent divide. You could arrange them so that part of the furniture screen could open into one area, and part into the other. Cover ugly backs of furniture with fabric or paper, or paint them to match the room.

A more flexible solution is to make a screen which can be pulled back when necessary (see page 41). Another possibility could be to hang light-weight curtains or vertical Venetian blinds from the ceiling.

This room has been split in half between the two windows, making the division seem more natural.

A curtain has been used to divide the two bedrooms. It can be left open, drawn half-way to provide some privacy, or right across to create two separate rooms.

The room on the left is arranged so that there is easy access to the room on the right.

Curtains divide each bedroom in two again, creating a bed area and desk area.

This cupboard acts as a barrier between the desk area and bedroom areas, it also provides storage for both areas.

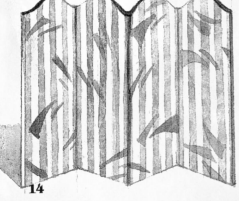

Creating a dining area

A permanent dining area is not often feasible in a room with limited space. A good solution is a drop-leaf table which can be used as a desk as well. Alternatively, look for a circular table that folds away. Garden tables are often designed like this and are relatively cheap. Remember though, that a plastic-topped table will not withstand hot dishes.

Canvas director's chairs make good additional seating and can be folded flat and hung on the wall when not in use.

If space is very short, you could install a flap-down table under a window-sill.

Soundproofing your room

Sound can travel very easily through walls and floorboards. To be fair to your family and neighbours, it is best to ensure that your room is well soundproofed if you plan to listen to or play loud music in it.

Floors

For a thorough solution, take floorboards up and put roof-insulating material between the joists. Then put down felt paper on top of the floorboards, a thick rubber underlay, a thick carpet, then rugs. If this is not possible, rubber flooring or cork tiles are the most sound proof floorings; put thick rugs on top of them.

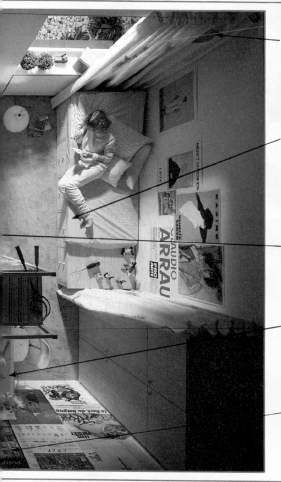

The curtains at the window are in the same fabric as the dividing curtains, adding continuity to the room design.

Drawers under the bed make the best possible use of space available for storage.

A table is placed in front of the cupboard to act as a further divide.

Each person has a desk light. They are operated separately from the bedroom lighting.

These posters pick up the colours and themes of each room. The central one is as a link between the two rooms.

Walls, ceilings and windows

Fix thick insulating board on to the walls using 5cm x 5cm battens screwed into the wall, then tuck roof insulating material into the gap behind. Cover this cladding with window-dressing felt*. Built-in cupboards backing on to this help to insulate walls even more. If this is not possible, use cork wall tiles to help deaden sound, or use felt as an alternative to wallpaper.

Ceilings can be tented with fabric or felt which has padding behind it (see page 4 for how to do it).

For maximum soundproofing, windows should be double-glazed, then covered with heavy curtains.

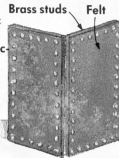

Brass studs   Felt

If only part of the room is used for music-making, the other half could be divided off with a screen made from insulation board.

Creating a bed/sitting room

If you are planning to use your bedroom as a sitting room as well, try to make it as uncluttered and impersonal as possible. *Futons* provide a good bed/sofa Alternatively, integrate your bed with the rest of your room by co-ordinating your bedcover and pillow covers with the curtain material.

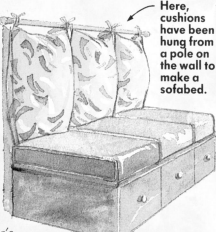

Here, cushions have been hung from a pole on the wall to make a sofabed.

Sharing your room

You can often avoid problems involved in sharing your room by thorough planning. Discuss your preferences with your room mate, and be prepared to compromise.

Where tastes conflict, try to find key areas which you agree about, such as a wallpaper border, stencilled *motif* or furnishing fabric. These common links can help to integrate two essentially different styles of *décor*.

* You can buy this from a shop fitter's.

Lighting

Good lighting can transform a room, giving it originality and style. You can use it to emphasize a favourite feature, make your room look larger, or create a cosy atmosphere.

Some forms of lighting are cheap to buy and simple to install. Others are expensive and need an electrician's help. What you decide to do will obviously depend on the fittings already available in your room, and on your budget.

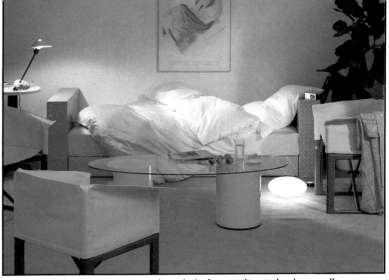

Here an anglepoise lamp provides a light for reading in bed, as well as additional background lighting. A stylish globe light creates an intimate atmosphere in the seating area.

Planning your room

Lighting must be practical as well as stylish. It is worth drawing a plan of your room's layout, to work out your lighting. The one on the right may give you some ideas. You will probably want a mixture of the following:

A. Background lighting. Soft, overall light.

B. Direct lighting. Lighting for specific tasks, such as reading.

C. Decorative lighting. Used to add shape to a room or draw attention to features.

Anglepoise reading lamp (B). Can be moved to shine on theatre posters (C).

Picture light (C).

Naked bulbs around mirror provide task lighting (B), as well as emphasizing theatrical theme (C).

Uplighter to illuminate plant (C), and for extra background lighting (A).

Table lamp for background lighting (A).

Shaping with light

To make your room appear larger:

★ Leave a gap between your furniture and the wall, and position uplighters in the gap.

★ Position a large mirror so that it reflects as much of your room as possible.

★ Direct light on to the ceiling to make it seem higher.

To create islands of light:

★ Point light away from the walls of your room, so that the boundaries are left undefined.

★ A dark lampshade with a light lining will create an attractive pool of light around it.

Positioning task lights

A badly positioned task light can do more harm than good. Here are a few tips.

Reading

☒ A central light is insufficient, and may cast shadows.

☑ Position a spotlight, wall light or lamp behind you.

Working

☒ A desk lamp positioned behind you throws your shadow on your work.

☑ Put it just in front of you, to the left.*

Storage

A light outside your cupboard casts shadows inside it. Striplights inside the cupboard make it easy to see inside.

Lighting fixtures

There are many different kinds of lighting fixtures on the market. Below are some of the most useful ones. There are also various types, styles and colours of bulb. Make sure you buy one which fits and has the right capacity for your light fitting. It should say on it what type it takes. Ask the sales assistant for advice, if you are in any doubt.

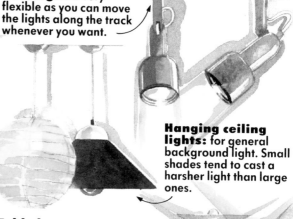
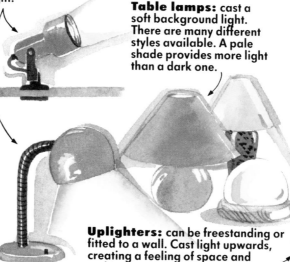

Eyeball spotlight: casts soft pools of light. Needs to be fitted by an electrician.

Lighting track and spotlights or floodlights: very flexible as you can move the lights along the track whenever you want.

Desk lamps: can be freestanding or clip-on. Most are adjustable so you can alter the fall of light.

Hanging ceiling lights: for general background light. Small shades tend to cast a harsher light than large ones.

Table lamps: cast a soft background light. There are many different styles available. A pale shade provides more light than a dark one.

Uplighters: can be freestanding or fitted to a wall. Cast light upwards, creating a feeling of space and making interesting shadows.

Novelty lights

You can create an impact by using unusual light fittings. Here are some ideas:

Chinese fan uplighter

Zig-zag lampstand

Fluorescent wall-lights

If you are left-handed, position it to the right.

A bout colour

The colours you choose for your room will play a large part in determining its mood and style. Your own response to different colours will depend on your taste.

Before you decide on a definite scheme, look at the next four pages to find out the basics of colour theory (the rules which govern the way colours work together).

Colour and form

Colour greatly affects the form of your room, that is, its basic shape and the 'landscape' made up by the objects in it. First, stand back and survey your room. What are its good and bad points? Is it big and empty or small and cluttered? Is it full of character or quite featureless?

Once you have decided on what you want to emphasize and what play down, you can use colour to bring about the transformation. On the right are some examples of what it can do:

Here, brightly painted furniture and woodwork liven up a dull room.

Camouflage. Dull or ugly items, such as pipes will seem to disappear if painted to match the walls.

Enhance features. Well-proportioned alcoves or an attractive fireplace look good picked out in a colour which contrasts with the background.

Create interest. If your room is just a square box, clever use of colour can add drama (see right).

In this alternative scheme, attention is focused on the walls and furnishing fabric.

Colour and proportion

Different colours have different effects on surfaces, making them appear to recede or advance. Warm, bright colours, such as red and orange make a room appear smaller, giving it a cosy feel. Cool, pale colours, such as blue and grey give a feeling of space. Clever use of bright and pale colours can visually alter the shape and proportions of your room. Below are some examples.

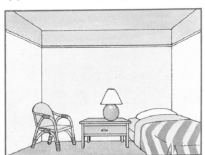

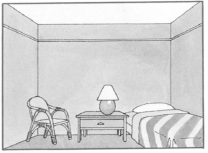

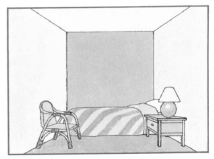

To make a tall ceiling look lower: colour it in a warm, advancing colour, such as pink. Use the same treatment for the walls above the level of the picture rail to extend the visual area of the ceiling.

To make a low ceiling look taller: colour it in a lighter value (*tone*) of the colour used for the walls. Take the colour of the walls right up to the level of the ceiling to reduce the visual area of the ceiling.

To make long, narrow areas seem wider: colour the two narrow ends in an advancing colour and the long walls in a lighter value (tone) of the same colour, place your furniture at right angles to the long walls.

Colour and pattern

Pattern works on surfaces in the same way as colour. Large, bold patterns advance and small, subtle patterns recede. The main colours in a pattern can accentuate or moderate its effect. For example, a large pattern in a warm, advancing colour may be overpowering but the same pattern in cooler *tones* would work well. Whilst colour only influences the mood of your room, pattern also contributes to its style.

Brightly coloured abstracts have a contemporary look.

Floral chintzes will give your room a cottagey feel.

Smaller flower prints look pretty and delicate.

Ethnic prints look good in vivid, strongly contrasting colours.

Rich, traditional designs will give an impression of opulence.

Nostalgic designs set a period style.

Fifties-style design

Art nouveau motif

Size and scale: it is important to relate the shape and size of a design to the shape and size of the area on which you are going to use it. On accessories such as cushion covers and curtain pelmets, use small-scale designs. Walls, full-length curtains, bedspreads and so on can usually take larger scale patterns.

Colour and texture

Different textured surfaces reflect light differently, and the amount of light which is reflected or absorbed by a surface affects its colour. For example, matt surfaces, such as a shaggy rug or brick walls, absorb light. This makes their colour look dark and rich. Shiny surfaces, such as gloss paint and silky-textured fabrics or wallpapers reflect light, making their colour appear brighter and paler.

If you want matt and shiny surfaces to match closely in colour, remember to take their texture into account when picking the exact *tone*. You can find out more about colour-matching over the page.

Like pattern, texture can emphasize the style of a room. For example, shiny textures such as steel, glass and mirrors give a room a modern, streamlined look, whilst brass looks cosier and more traditional. Richly textured surfaces, such as dhurries*, embroidered wall-hangings and batik fabric give a room an ethnic flavour.

* Dhurries are woven, Indian rugs.

The colour wheel

Choosing colours which go well together doesn't come naturally to everyone. Too many colours used together can look hectic, whereas too few may look dull.

A **monochromatic colour scheme** mixes various *tones* of one colour. Small touches of a contrasting colour (known as **accents**) will add interest to the scheme.

Opposite colours (such as yellow and purple) will give you a contrasting, complementary colour scheme.

Adjacent colours on the wheel, such as turquoise, blue and green create a harmonious effect.

Creating a mood

Colours from the middle bands of the wheel are brightest. They create a stimulating mood, so are good for study areas.

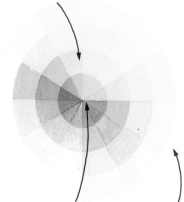

Colours from the centre of the wheel are darkest. The warm ones create an intimate mood, so are good for social areas.

Colours from the outer band are palest. Cool or neutral ones create a restful mood, so are good for relaxing and sleeping areas.

Look at the way colours relate to each other on the wheel above. Opposites or neighbours on the colour wheel generally work better together than a random choice. Each segment of the wheel is graded by *tone* – dark at the centre, becoming lighter at the edges.

Colour schemes

The most successful colour schemes have an inspired touch. Looking at paint charts and shop catalogues may tempt you to pick a ready-made scheme. If you want something more original, look around you at the different colour combinations you see every day and think about how you respond to them.

Before making your final choice, it is important to make sure your proposed scheme is a practical choice which fits in with your budget and day-to-day needs.

Inspiration

Finding inspiration for a colour scheme is easy – just look around you. The still life opposite shows how even the most unusual objects can inspire a successful scheme. Notice your response to the colours and *tones* you see every day and if there are certain combinations which you always seem to be drawn to, choose these colours for your room.

In this room, the colours of the walls and the curtain fabric were inspired by the green and terracotta of the vases.

Natural things can provide a good basis for a harmonious scheme.

A permanent fixture, such as a carpet, or ceramic tiles, can provide a practical basis for your colour scheme.

Fabric can be a good source of ideas. Here for example, the orange and blue of the curtains sets the scheme for the room.

A theme chosen from a book, an exhibition or a foreign holiday can inspire your colour scheme.

Here, for example, the theme of night has been chosen. The tones of blue and black and the soft glow cast by the uplighter create a mysterious atmosphere.

Budgeting

If you are very lucky, you may be able to redecorate your room from scratch, which gives you complete freedom of choice when choosing colours. However, limited funds mean most people have to work around certain items which they cannot afford to replace, such as a carpet, soft furnishings, or a sofabed.

You can either choose a colour scheme which complements the existing items, or you can devise a totally new one, disguising the permanent fixtures cheaply.

There are some ideas for ways to do this on pages 4-7.

Time-scale

It is worth considering the long-term consequences of living with your choice of colour scheme – what strikes you as irresistible now, might seem old fashioned in six month's time.

If you are going to change a major item, such as a carpet, remember that it may have to see you through several changes of *décor* in future. A versatile neutral, such as beige or grey is probably safest.

If you want to keep up with the latest colours, use them sparingly and on smaller items, which will not be so costly to replace.

Wear and tear

Wear and tear can wreak havoc on your colour scheme. A cream carpet can turn muddy grey in a matter of weeks (unless you ban outdoor shoes from the room). A navy blue duvet cover could well look like a shadow of its former self after a few washes.

Be sure to bear in mind the functions of different objects in your room as well as their decorative properties when choosing their colours.

When buying fabric, carpet, wallpaper and so on, it is important to buy the right type and weight for the area you want to cover.

Colour matching

Even the most experienced interior designer cannot remember colours exactly. The range of *tones* available in just one colour can be very confusing when you are trying to match fabric to paint, or carpet to wallpaper.

To save making expensive mistakes, it is a good idea to make yourself a sample board. This is a clip-board, or piece of stiff card to which you attach swatches, paint charts and samples when shopping for materials.

Ask the shop assistant for samples of any materials which you like the look of*. Before buying final quantities of anything, take the samples home and look at them in your room, by daylight and artificial light.

If you want to match new items to old, try to find offcuts, left over when the old items were bought, and clip these to your board.

Remember that different textures absorb light differently. Bear this in mind when matching dull textures to shiny ones.

To make a choice between several possible fabrics, clip samples on to your board for easy comparison.

A sample board

* If you cannot get a sample from the shop, note the reference number and colour of the range and write to the manufacturer for a sample.

Wallpapering

Papering your room is a simple and cheap way to give the walls a patterned or textured finish. It is also very satisfying to do. The choice of styles available is vast (there are some examples below). To find out how much paper to buy, turn to page 54.

Types of wallpaper

Lining paper. Makes an uneven surface smooth. Comes in different weights. Can be painted or papered over.

Standard wallpaper. Available in many weights, patterns and colours. Suitable for bedrooms and living rooms.

Washable wallpaper. Has waterproof finish, so may be sponged clean.

Textured relief paper. Types include woodchip (random pattern), contoured and blown vinyls (relief patterns) and embossed papers. Good for poor surfaces. Some are ready coloured, others must be painted.

Vinyl. Hard-wearing, washable finish. Comes ready-pasted and unpasted. More costly than standard paper.

Foamed polyethylene. Lightweight paper with a smooth finish. A good insulator and warm to the touch. Paste the wall to hang.

In this small room, the bright wallpaper works well because the pattern is small and subtle.

Pattern and colour

When choosing paper, think about the size and shape of your room and the effect you want to create.

★Big rooms look cosier decorated with large, bold patterns. In a small room, try using a large pattern in pale colours or a small one in bold colours. Large, bold patterns may be overpowering in a small room.

★A low or sloping ceiling will seem to recede if papered to match the walls, in a small or light-coloured pattern.

★If your room has a specific problem, such as lack of light, think about how your choice of wallpaper might improve it.

★Consider any other areas of texture and pattern in your room. If you have already bought fabric, carpet or paint, choose a wallpaper which goes well with it.

This boldly-patterned, multi-coloured paper would be a good alternative for the same room, as it is light in *tone*.

Using borders

Below are some ideas for combining wallpapers and borders to stylish effect.

Paper up to door height, border, paint above.

Paper up to waist height, border, paint above.

Bold paper to waist height, border, subtle paper above.

Pattern matching

Papers with a regular pattern sequence need to be carefully matched at the seams to preserve the continuity of the design. Remember to allow for the wastage this entails when estimating quantities (see page 54).

Preparation

It is best to strip and prepare your walls before choosing a new wallpaper, as you may find a poor surface underneath, which requires lining or a textured paper to conceal it.

1. Clear the room and cover the floor with dust sheets.

2. Strip the wall with a scraper (see page 58). If the paper won't come off easily, dampen the surface (take care not to wet sockets or switches).

3. Fill any cracks in the plaster with filler and smooth with sandpaper when dry.

4. Paint the woodwork, then paint any areas which you are not going to paper. You can find out how to do this on page 27.

5. Set up the pasting table, mix your paste and gather together all your equipment.

Equipment checklist

- Plumb bob, chalk and sticky tape
- Wallpaper paste
- Pasting brush and wallpapering brush
- Wallpaper scissors and trimming knife
- Retractable rule
- Pasting table
- Step ladder
- String (if using plain paper)

Hanging patterned paper

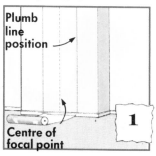

1. First, chalk a mark at the centre of the focal point of your room. Measure half the width of your wallpaper and make a mark that distance from your first one.

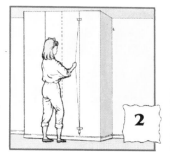

2. Rub chalk into the plumb bob string and tape it to the wall. Drop weighted end and tape in place. Snap the string against the wall. Remove the plumb bob.

3. Add 10cm to the height of your wall, and cut a sheet of paper to the total length. Align a second sheet next to the first and cut. Repeat with enough sheets for one wall*.

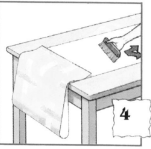

4. Place the paper on the table. Paste it from the centre outwards. If the table is too short, fold the paper as shown and let it hang over the edge while you paste the rest.

5. Fold the pasted ends of the paper inwards, leaving a gap in the middle. Holding the paper as shown, position yourself on the ladder, within reach of the top of the wall.

6. Unfold the top half of the sheet. With an overlap of 5cm at the top of the wall, align the side with the plumb line. Gently brush in place, from the centre out.

7. To trim the top edge, press the paper into the angle of the wall. Peel it off and cut along the fold. Smooth the paper back down. Repeat for the lower edge.

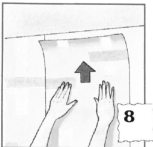

8. Work outwards in both directions, hanging the next sheet in the same way as the first. Ease it alongside the first, until the pattern matches.

Hanging plain or matchless paper

Measure the wall and add 10cm. Cut a piece of string to the total length. Using this as a measure, cut enough paper for the first wall. Start by a door or window, marking a plumb line one sheet of wallpaper's width from the frame. Paste and hang the paper as shown above. Repeat with the next sheet, working away from the light. Turn over to find out how to cope with obstacles.

*Number each sheet and, if the pattern is directional, mark 'top' on the back.

Coping with obstacles

Internal and external corners

1. Trim the sheet of paper so that it overlaps the corner by about 2cm. Paste and hang it as normal. Then mark a plumb line on the new wall, as before (see page 23).

2. Hang the next sheet of paper, aligning it with your plumb line on one side and allowing the other edge to overlap the previous sheet, making a neat finish in the corner.

Electrical fittings

1. Turn off the electricity at the mains. Loosely unscrew the socket or switch plate. Paste and hang the paper, pressing down gently over the fitting, to reveal its outline.

2. With a trimming knife, make diagonal cuts across the centre of the fitting, as shown. Trim the flaps to 1cm. Tuck them behind the fitting* and screw it back in place. Wipe off any paste.

Radiators

1. Hold a length of wallpaper over the top of the radiator. Mark the height and position of the brackets in chalk. Starting at the bottom, cut the paper along the chalk marks.

2. Then make two short, horizontal cuts above and below the bracket area, as shown. This helps the paper to lie flat behind the radiator. Paste and hang the paper as normal.

Window recesses

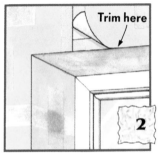

1. First paper the recess, trimming each sheet of paper so that it overlaps the wall by about 2cm, as shown. Then paste and hang a sheet of paper to overlap the recess.

2. Press the paper gently around the corner of the recess. Then peel it back and trim carefully along the crease, as shown. Continue in the same way until the entire recess is papered.

Door frames

1. From a vantage point on your ladder, hold a length of paper over the door frame. Mark in chalk where the door frame comes. Trim inside the marks, leaving a 2cm allowance.

2. Paste and hang the paper as normal. Press down gently so that the outline of the door frame is visible. Then make a small, diagonal cut away from the corner of the frame.

3. Now press the 2cm allowance into the angle where the wall meets the door frame. Peel back the overlap and cut along the fold. Press the trimmed edge down neatly.

Practical tips

If you find an air bubble in a sheet of paper which is already in position, leave it for 24 hours as it may dry flat. If not, cut a cross through the centre of the bubble with your trimming knife. Lift the flaps and dab a little paste under each one. Finally smooth them back down.

Do not do this with metallic paper, as it can conduct electricity.

Adding a border

Borders are useful for covering less than perfect edges, whether they occur where the wall meets the ceiling, at waist height, or at picture rail level.

Borders also add style and definition to a room. If you are using a border which has a repeating pattern sequence, centre the pattern at the focal point of your room (as for wallpaper, see page 23) and work outwards.

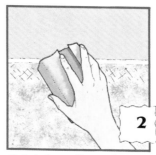

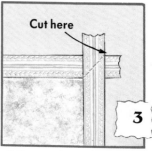

1. Measure from the floor to the level you want a border and mark with chalk. Hold a spirit level on the mark and chalk along it. Repeat along the length of the wall. Join up the lines with a metre rule.

2. Rub the wallpaper lightly with sandpaper where the border will overlap it. This helps it to stick. Paste the border and fix it in place on your guideline. Wipe off any excess paste.

3. For a right angle join, overlap the ends of the border. With a trimming knife, cut diagonally through both layers. Peel back ends, remove the loose bits and press ends back down.

Lining your wall

Lining your wall is a good idea if it has a very uneven surface. If you are going to paint over lining paper, hang it vertically. If you are going to wallpaper over the top of it, hang the lining paper horizontally. This prevents the vertical joints of the two layers from coinciding. Hang the lining paper using the same technique as for vertical hanging, starting at the top of the wall.

Alternatives to wallpaper

There are many other ways to decorate your walls with pattern and texture, ranging from fabric wall coverings which are bonded on to paper and hung like wallpaper, to original collages.

Hessian comes with a paper or latex backing, in a range of colours. You can buy natural-coloured hessian cloth cheaply from an upholsterer.

Fabric gives a room an intimate, luxurious feel, but costs more than wallpaper. It can be attached flat, using a staple gun, or pleated, hung on wooden battens. ▼

Comics, newspapers or postcards ▲ can make a quirky alternative to wallpaper. In a small room, they may be rather overpowering on every surface and would be better reserved for an alcove or single wall.

Wood panelling. This can look very impressive, but is rather expensive to have installed. Wood is a good insulator and sound-proofer.

Cork is available on a paper ▲ backing and provides a warm, interestingly textured surface which insulates the room well. Cork is difficult to hang and wears fairly quickly.

Collage. This is a picture made from scrap paper, old magazines, fabric etc. Plan your design on paper first, then draw up a simplified version on the wall in chalk.

U sing paint

Here, light flat colour gives an impression of space. The shelves are picked out in a darker shade, making a feature of the triangular alcove.

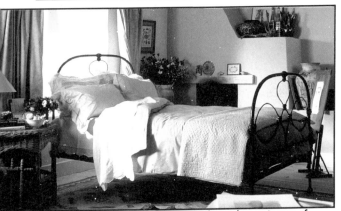

In this room, different colours mark out the various surfaces. The scheme works because the colours used are all of a similar depth of *tone*.

This geometric pattern is done with flat colour. First, a *base coat* is painted, and the pattern drawn on the wall and masked with tape. Then each colour in turn is applied and allowed to dry.

You can change the look of a room more easily with paint and lighting than with any amount of expensive furniture and ornaments. Paint can transform almost any surface, from walls and ceilings to radiators and floors. On the next eight pages you will find many different paint techniques, ranging from *flat colour* to textured effects, stencils and murals. The chart on page 53 tells you all about the properties of paint and its suitability for different surfaces.

Flat colour

Flat colour is a single shade of paint, applied evenly over a surface. This need not result in a boring effect. On the right are some examples of the ways in which you can use it.

Types of paint

Oil based paint gives a tough, water-resistant surface. For a shiny finish, suitable for woodwork, choose gloss. For a finish with a slight sheen, suitable for walls or woodwork, choose eggshell paint. Gloss comes in liquid or non-drip form. The consistency of eggshell is a cross between matt and gloss. Oil-based paints need an *undercoat* – use one which is made by the same manufacturer as the *top coat*.

Emulsion or water-based paint comes in silk (slightly shiny) or matt finish (dull) and in liquid or solid form. Emulsion is quick-drying and washable. It is usually used for walls and ceilings.

Buying your paint

You should be able to find the colour you want, however unusual or specific. If it does not appear on a shade card for ready-mixed paint, try one of the ranges of colours which can be mixed on request at large hardware stores. If you find it hard to visualize your room in a different colour, you can buy small sample pots of paint very cheaply which enable you to try out one or more colours, before buying a larger quantity. See how the colour looks in daylight and artificial light, before making a final decision.

Applying flat colour

Using a roller and tray (for emulsion only). First use a brush to paint the edges and corners of the surface. Then pour a little paint into the deep end of the tray. Dip in the roller and run it over the ridged area of the tray until evenly coated.

Paint a small area of the surface at a time, using criss-cross diagonal strokes at first, then vertical ones, to give a neat finish. When you move to the next area, neaten the join by painting over it with vertical strokes.

Using a brush (for all types of paint). Load the brush evenly. Paint a small area at a time, making your strokes vertical and horizontal by turns*.

*For skirting boards, use horizontal strokes only.
** For a flush door, paint the sides first, then the front, working from the top down.

Equipment checklist

- Paint
- Primer or undercoat (if painting a new surface)
- Clean rags
- 2.5cm brush for small areas, 7cm brush for large areas and 1.9cm cutting-in brush for windows
- Sugar soap or detergent
- Masking tape
- Dust sheets
- Step ladder
- White spirit (for gloss only)
- Roller and tray (optional, for emulsion only)

Preparation

Paint your room when you will be able to leave it empty to dry (to allow the fumes to disperse). Work in the light and cover the floor with dust sheets. Paint the walls or ceiling first, then the woodwork.

Wallpaper can often be painted. Test a patch which won't show to see if it runs, or absorbs the paint. If there is a problem, strip the walls. If not, clean them before you start.

Old paint can usually be painted. First clean the walls with sugar soap and rinse.

An uneven surface should be lined or covered with textured paper before painting. If the plaster has just a few cracks in, fill them and sandpaper before painting.

A new surface, such as bare wood or fresh plaster, needs primer and/or undercoat (see the chart on page 53).

Painting different surfaces

Walls. Paint around all the edges, doors and windows with a small brush. Fill in using a large brush or roller, starting at the window and painting away from the light.

Ceilings. Paint around the edges of the ceiling with a small brush. Then paint in parallel strips, starting at the window wall and moving away from the light.

Casement windows. Mask glass and remove handles. Open window and paint in the order marked one to six above. Finally paint the sill and surround.

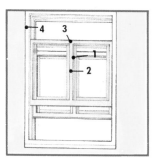

Sash windows. Mask glass. Position sashes as shown. Paint areas one to three. Reverse sashes and paint the rest. Then paint the frame. Leave to dry. Paint area four.

Panel doors**. Wedge the door open and remove the handle. First, paint area one. Then paint areas two to twelve, as shown. Finally, paint the door frame.

Practical tips

★To prevent the bristles of your paint brush from drying up between painting sessions, wrap them in cling film.

★To stop bristles splaying when painting straight lines, wrap an elastic band around the ends.

Decorative paint effects

Paint does not have to be applied as a single *flat colour*. It can also be used in a number of decorative ways to add interest and texture to different surfaces, such as walls and furniture.

You can create interesting and unusual effects by combining two or more colours, or *tones* of the same colour. The techniques vary in difficulty and sophistication, from random spattering to precise simulation of real marble. Start with a simple technique on a large surface. Opposite are three simple methods for you to try.

Equipment checklist

- Stepladder
- Dust sheets (to protect floor)
- 10cm paint brush
- Roller and tray
- Kitchen towel or rags
- Water
- White spirit
- Sandpaper
- Emulsion paint (for walls)
- Eggshell paint (for wood and metal)
- Natural sponge (for sponging)
- Shallow dish (for sponging)
- Wooden ruler (for spattering)
- Small paint brush (for spattering)
- Decorator's comb (for combing)

Sponging adds texture to this subtle colour scheme. It can also be used to disguise uneven walls.

Here, surfaces spattered with blue and white create a striking random, speckled effect.

Here, wood-panelled walls have been combed in light grey, giving them a soft, textured look.

Sponging walls

1. Choose two colours that go well together (one should be darker than the other). Thin each one with a little water. With the lighter colour, apply an even coat of paint to the wall using a brush or roller. Leave to dry.

Spattering walls

1. Choose one colour for your *base coat* and two or three contrasting colours. Thin each one with a little water. Using a large brush or roller, paint the wall with the base coat. Leave until thoroughly dry.

Combing wood

1. Decide what colour you want the woodwork to be. Choose two shades of that colour — one light and one dark. Thin each one with a little white spirit. Then smooth down your surface with sandpaper and wipe clean.

2. Wet a natural sponge with water, then wring it out so that it is only slightly damp. Carefully pour a small amount of the darker paint into a shallow dish or paint tray. Dip the sponge in the paint and blot on a rag.

3. Starting in a corner, dab the sponge on to the wall, rotating it occasionally to vary the pattern. Continue until the whole wall is covered, applying paint to the sponge whenever the print begins to fade.

2. Dip a small paint brush into the first of your two colours, making sure that only the tips of the bristles are covered. Gently tap the brush against the inner rim of the paint tin to remove any excess paint.

3. Hold a ruler a little distance* from the wall. Tap the brush handle against it so that the paint showers the wall. Continue until the wall is completely spattered. Leave to dry before repeating with the next colour.

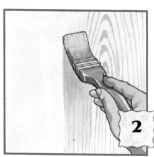

2. Using a large paint brush, apply an even coat of the lighter of your two shades, following the grain of the wood. Leave until thoroughly dry. Carefully apply a thin layer of your darker shade in the same way.

3. While the **top coat** is still wet, drag a decorator's comb through the paint to reveal lines of the lighter **base coat.** Use a rag to wipe the comb clean now and then, to prevent it becoming clogged with paint.

Other paint techniques

Each of the following techniques has been coded according to difficulty: ★ (easy) ★★ (fairly easy) ★★★ (hard).

Marbling. This simulates real marble. It is created by painting on patches of colour and blending them together. Thin veins are then added with a brush or feather.

★★★

Rag-rolling. This effect is produced by painting on a light **base coat**, letting it dry, then covering it with a darker **top coat**. A rag is then rolled over the wet surface to expose the lighter colour.

★★

Stippling. This is done by applying two coats of paint as for rag-rolling. The pattern is made by stabbing the wet **top coat** repeatedly with a stiff-bristled brush.

★

Cissing or fossilizing. Small patches of colour are painted on and blended together. These are spattered with white spirit and paint, then fine veins are added.

★★★

Tortoiseshelling. Patches of colour are painted on to a surface, then blended together. Darker shapes are added and softened with a dry brush. The surface is then spattered with white spirit and blended as before.

★★★

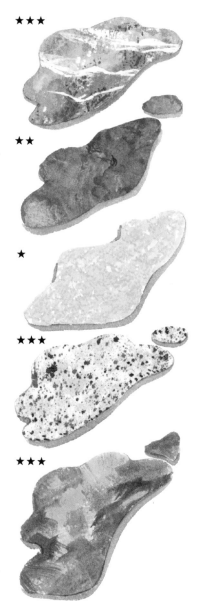

Practical tips

★If you are attempting a new technique or are unsure about the colours you have chosen**, buy some cheap lining paper and experiment before you start on walls or woodwork.

★Always keep some paper towels or old rags by your side when working, to remove any excess paint from your brush or sponge. A build-up of paint can create a clumsy effect.

* The further away you hold your ruler, the subtler the effect will be.
** If you do not feel confident about choosing contrasting colours, use different **tones** of the same colour.

S tencilling

A stencil is a guide which you can use to paint a simple image on a flat surface. A stencilled pattern can make the difference between a tasteful room and one which is really stylish.

You could use stencils to draw attention to an attractive feature, such as a window, or cornice. If your room is plain, you could add interest by stencilling a border around it, or by stencilling a *motif* on furniture or fabric.

There is a wide range of stencil designs available in the shops, but it is more economical, and very satisfying, to design your own. Here you can find out how.

Here a simple art deco-style stencil emphasizes the period feel of the room.

Making stencils

You will need to make a separate stencil for each colour separation (see right), unless your design has only one colour.

Equipment checklist

- Acetate*
- Masking tape
- Permanent marker
- Tracing paper
- Pencil
- Cutting mat
- Craft knife

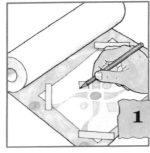

1. Tape your original image on a flat surface. Lay tracing paper on top and secure with masking tape. Trace the design in as much detail as you like. Plan a colour scheme.

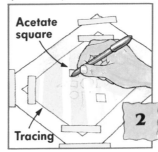

2. Cut an acetate square for each colour in your design. Tape down your tracing. Lay the first square on it. Trace a solid line in marker around the area of your first colour.

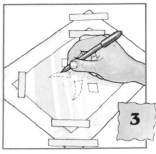

3. Trace a dotted line over the areas of your other colours. On the next square, trace the area of your second colour in solid line and use dotted line for the rest, and so on.

Applying stencils

Equipment checklist

- Stencil paints
- Stencil brushes (one for each colour)
- Old saucers
- Paper towel
- Detergent
- Pencil
- White spirit
- Tracing paper
- Steel ruler
- Jam jars
- Elastic bands
- Low-tack tape*
- Scrap paper

Preparation

First, draw a positioning guide. For a single image, centre your stencil on the surface. For a border, mark a guideline with a spirit level**. Centre the stencil on the line, then work outwards.

1. Collect all your equipment together. Carefully align the stencil for your first colour with your positioning guideline (see left) and secure it around the edges with low-tack tape.

2. Pour a little of your first colour into a saucer. Dip the tip of your brush into the paint and blot it on the paper towel. Now try it out on scrap paper to make sure it is almost dry.

Stencilling on different surfaces

You can stencil on to walls, floors, furniture and fabrics. To co-ordinate the contents of your room, you could adapt one stencil design to suit different areas. You can stencil on matt surfaces using emulsion, but you will get a bolder result if you use special stencil paints or crayons which can be used on any surface except high gloss. For stencilling fabric, you will need to use special fabric paints.

This stencil is reproduced on page 50 for you to copy.

Designing stencils

A stencil which you have designed yourself will make your room unique. For inspiration, look at fabric and wallpaper, books, postcards etc. Choose stylized images which can easily be broken down into basic shapes. You can find out how to make stencils below.

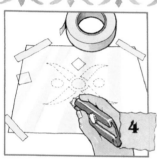

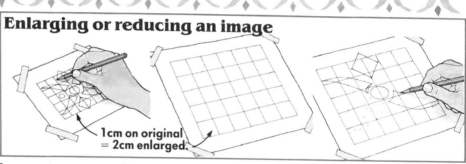

Enlarging or reducing an image

1cm on original = 2cm enlarged.

4. When you have finished, tape the first sheet of acetate to your cutting mat and carefully cut around the solid line with your craft knife. Repeat with each sheet.

Tape your image on to a flat surface. In pencil draw a grid of 1cm squares on it. On a new piece of paper draw a square the size you want, in proportion to your original.

Divide it into the same number of squares as your original, making the squares proportionally bigger, if enlarging, or smaller, if reducing your image.

Carefully plot the points on your new grid where the image outline crosses the squares of your old grid. Now join up the dots, until you have redrawn the whole image.

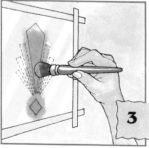

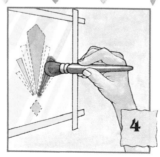

Practical tips

★A good alternative to using a stencilling brush is to apply paint from a spray can. Mask the surrounding area with newspaper before you start.

★You can buy metallic paint in pots or aerosols which looks particularly effective if used against a dark background.

3. Holding the brush at right angles to the surface, dab the paint very lightly through the cut-out, using a circular motion. Strengthen the colour very gradually*, until you achieve the effect you want.

4. Unless you are stencilling a repeat pattern**, remove the first stencil and tape the next one in its place, using your pencil marks as a guide. With a new brush, dab on the second colour, as before.

5. Continue until you have completed the stencil in every colour. When you have finished, clean your stencils and brushes. Wrap elastic bands around the tips of the brushes, to keep them straight.

* To give your stencil a 3-dimensional effect, deepen the colour towards the centre of your stencil.
** If doing a repeat pattern, stencil the whole sequence in one colour before going back to start the next.

Murals

Murals are images painted directly on to a wall or ceiling. You can paint a mural of anything you like, from simple abstracts to complex, realistic scenes. Do not worry if you lack confidence as an artist as many of the techniques shown here are easy to do, yet very effective.

You can use murals to add character to a featureless room, brighten up a dark corner or disguise an awkward space. Geometric patterns are particularly effective for decorating a room which is furnished in a contemporary style.

This appealing mural shows that a good idea, however simple, can be just as effective as an artistic masterpiece.

Planning a mural

Although the size and shape of your mural will largely depend on the space available, you need to think carefully about your choice of subject.

For inspiration, look at books, magazines and postcards. Pick fairly simple images. Two-dimensional pictures are ideal as they use shape and colour rather than complicated shading and *perspective*.

Try to link your mural with the rest of your room. The easiest way to do this is through your choice of colours or by continuing the theme on smaller items in the room, such as blinds. If your room already has a theme, for example sport, choose a subject that reflects this.

These designs can be enlarged to fit your wall. Turn to page 50, where they are drawn to scale.

Equipment checklist

- Emulsion paint (for large areas)
- Acrylic or emulsion* paint (for small areas)
- Paint brushes (various sizes)
- Roller and tray (for large areas)
- Artist's brush
- Plumb bob
- Ruler
- Chalk
- Paper
- Pencil
- Set square
- Dust sheets

Preparation

A mural should ideally be painted directly on to a bare wall. You will need to remove any existing wallpaper before starting (see page 52). Fill any cracks and sand the surface smooth.

If the surface is particularly bad you can cover the wall with lining paper, but make sure the seams match perfectly.

An *undercoat* of white emulsion provides a good, neutral base.

* When using small amounts of emulsion paint, see if trial size pots are available in your chosen colours.

Drawing a freehand image

If you are fairly confident about your drawing ability, you can sketch a scene or pattern directly on to the wall. Use chalk or charcoal, as these can easily be rubbed out with a damp cloth, if you make a mistake.

When drawing on the wall it is a good idea to stand back now and again to check that your sketch looks right from a distance. If you are repeating a pattern or simple image you can save time by making a **template** to draw around.

Enlarging an image from a plan

If you find it difficult to draw directly on to a wall, you can design your own mural and then enlarge it by using a plan. Divide the wall into equal squares. Use a plumb line to mark in each vertical line, then draw in the horizontals with a set square and ruler. Next draw a small grid on a piece of paper with the same number of squares. Sketch your design

on to it. Then transfer it to the wall square-by-square.

If you prefer you can enlarge a picture from a magazine or book. To do this, draw a grid over the image (see page 31) before transferring it, square by square, to a larger grid on the wall. Choose a picture of similar proportions to your wall or one that can be adapted.

Painting a mural

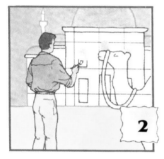

1. Working from the top of your wall downwards, begin with larger areas, such as the sky. Carefully outline one section using a small brush. With a large brush or roller, fill it in and leave until thoroughly dry.

2. Continue painting each section using a different brush/roller for each colour.* Avoid painting an area next to one that is still drying, as you could smudge it or find that the two colours run together.

3. Leave the mural to dry. You can then neaten rough edges using an artist's brush and add fine details, such as small areas of **accent colour**. Finally, rub out any grid marks that may still be visible around the mural.

Trompe l'oeil

Trompe l'oeil is a french term which means 'to deceive the eye'. It is used to describe an image which is so life-like that it looks real. Architectural features are a common subject in trompe l'oeil murals.

Trompe l'oeil effects require quite a lot of artistic skill. To create an impression of three dimensions, objects need to be drawn in **perspective**, with highlights and shading to make them look solid. Begin by choosing something fairly simple such as an ornament on a shelf or plants growing up from the skirting board. You can make an illusion even more convincing by combining real objects with painted items.

Practical tips

★Stippling (see page 29) is a useful technique for adding texture to large areas of **flat colour** such as sky.

★Sponging (see pages 28-29) is a quick and effective way of suggesting foliage.

★Stencilling (see pages 30-31) is a useful short cut when adding simple details such as flowers, or birds in flight.

★To create a silhouette, place an object, or ask a friend to stand in front of a light. This will cast a shadow on the wall which you can draw around and then paint.

★If you don't like freehand drawing, use a slide projecter to project your favourite slide on to your wall. Trace around the outline, then paint to match the original.

A combination of real fixtures and painted images creates a convincing illusion.

* Alternatively, wash your brush/roller thoroughly before applying a new colour.

Curtains and blinds

Although most people realise the practical need for curtains and blinds, many forget about their decorative possibilities. Each is an important styling device and integral part of a room's *décor*. Used cleverly, they can enhance architectural features, disguise flaws and ugly views, or provide an eye-catching feature in a room which would otherwise be ordinary.

Practical planning

Privacy. When a room is lit at night, some blinds and unlined curtains become see-through, from the outside looking in. Combining curtains and blinds provides a versatile solution to this problem. If your room is overlooked, venetian blinds or café curtains (which cover the lower half of the window) are a good option for the daytime.

Daylight. To maximize daylight, choose blinds, as these obscure the least light when not in use. To soften harsh light, filter daylight through thin fabric, venetian or bamboo blinds.

Warmth. Heavy, lined curtains provide insulation. Alternatively, use blinds and light curtains together.

Co-ordinating your look

A bright red venetian blind complements this clean, geometric look.

Choose a style that reflects the theme of your room. For example, venetian blinds will complement a *hi-tech* room. Long, heavy curtains suit formal surroundings, and Austrian blinds work well in prettier, more delicate rooms.

Clever use of texture can enhance the mood of your room. Textured fabrics create a warm, cosy atmosphere; smooth or shiny fabrics tend to look colder.

Look for colours that match the accessories in your room or pick out a particular *accent colour*.

Here, a subtle floral print has been used to create a cosy, cottagey feel.

Curtain treatments

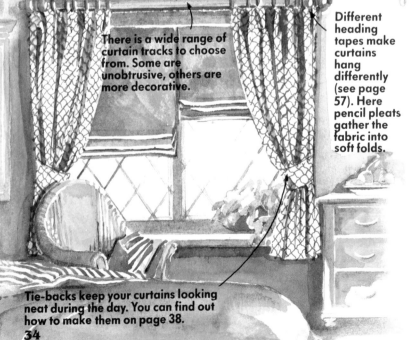

There is a wide range of curtain tracks to choose from. Some are unobtrusive, others are more decorative.

Different heading tapes make curtains hang differently (see page 57). Here pencil pleats gather the fabric into soft folds.

Tie-backs keep your curtains looking neat during the day. You can find out how to make them on page 38.

Types of blind

Roller blinds are flat pieces of fabric which roll up around wooden dowelling.

Roman blinds are flat pieces of fabric with vertical lengths of tape attached to the back. These gather the blind into smooth horizontal pleats.

Austrian (or festoon) blinds are gathered along the top edge in the same way as a curtain. Vertical lengths of tape gather the blind into wide *ruches*.

Venetian blinds are made from horizontal strips of metal or plastic held together with fine cord.

Bamboo blinds are made from thin strips of bamboo sewn together.

Making your own curtains and blinds

It is simple and very economical to make your own curtains and blinds.

Buying fabric

★To estimate the amount of fabric you need for curtains, see page 56. For blinds, read the instructions with your kit.

★Choose curtain or furnishing fabrics (see page 56). Dress fabric may not hang correctly and fades easily.

★Take samples home to check that the colour and weight are right.

★Always check the cleaning instructions*

Simple lined curtains

Equipment checklist

- Dressmaker's scissors
- Heading tape
- Curtain fabric
- Lining
- Matching sewing thread
- Contrasting tacking thread
- Pins
- Sewing machine
- Iron

1. Decide how much fabric you need (see page 56). Once you have decided the length of each curtain, add an additional 5cm for the hem and 2.5cm for the heading. Carefully cut both lining and curtain fabric.

2. If using more than one width of fabric for each curtain, match any pattern along the sewing line. With right sides together, pin and stitch in place. To neaten raw edges, turn in 5mm and stitch. Join lining in the same way.

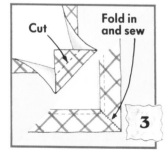

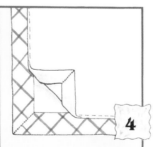

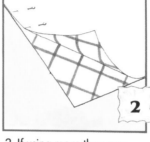

3. To neaten the sides of each curtain, turn in about 1.5cm and sew down each side. Stop 5cm from the bottom. Turn up your hem and sew in place, leaving 5cm either end. *Mitre* each corner as shown. Iron the curtain.

4. With wrong sides facing, lay curtain and lining on the floor. Neaten the sides of the lining so that the outside edges slightly overlap the hemmed edges of the curtain. Hem the bottom in the same way. Sew and mitre.

5. With wrong sides facing, match the top edges of the curtain and lining. Pin and tack together, then fold over on to the lining so that 2.5cm of the curtain is visible. Pin heading tape to it and sew as shown.

Making blinds

You can make Austrian, Roman or roller blinds using your own material and a ready-bought kit. Kits come in several sizes which can be adapted to fit most windows. Each kit contains all the fittings you need and step-by-step instructions. You can buy them from specialist shops and department stores.

* Cleaning instructions are often printed on the selvedge (edge of the fabric).

Practical tips

★ To make a short window appear longer, attach your curtain track some distance above the window and hang full-length curtains.

★To make a window look wider, extend your curtain track at either side of the window. When pulled back the curtains hang against the wall, not the window.

★If your window is too wide, attach a track of the same width. When pulled back, the curtains will obscure a portion of the window.

★Curtains that meet permanently in the middle reduce the width of the window. The curtains can be tied back during the day.

★If your window is too long, obscure the top of the window using a pelmet or valance.

★Use café curtains, lace or venetian blinds to disguise an ugly view.

★Full length curtains which have vertical stripes will make your room look higher.

★Sill length curtains with a horizontal pattern will reduce the height of your room.

★If you have a window that is situated in an awkward corner, use a simple blind or a single curtain which can be drawn or folded back during the day.

Soft furnishings

Changing the soft furnishings in your room is a good way to revamp its image without spending a fortune. For example, an unconventional choice of fabric for a duvet cover and pillow cases can make your bed a dramatic feature. Loose covers will give a new lease of life to old or unattractive chairs. To achieve a co-ordinated look, choose the same colour fabric, for the chair covers and bed linen.

Below you can find out how to make some basic soft furnishings and over the page are ideas for accessories which will give your room a touch of luxury.

Here, bed linen has been co-ordinated using bright, geometric fabric. Decorative borders and smocking add interest to the pillow cases.

Equipment checklist

- Fabric
- Matching thread (for sewing)
- Contrasting thread (for tacking)
- Dressmaker's scissors
- Tape measure
- Sewing machine (preferably with a zig-zag foot attachment)
- Iron and ironing board
- Fastening tape
- Pins

Bed linen

Ready-made bed linen is expensive and usually only available in a limited range of colours and patterns. Making your own gives you a wider choice. You can buy special, wide fabric called *sheeting* or join together ordinary lengths of fabric*. Remember to allow 1.5cm extra for each seam and to buy more if pattern matching. Look for easy-care, crease resistant fabrics.

Loose sheets and bedspreads

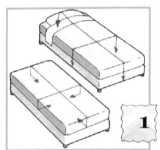

1. **For sheets:** measure your bed (see blue lines above). Allow 180cm to tuck under. **For covers:** measure the bed and pillow (see green lines). Add 4cm (for hems) to all measurements.

2. Cut your fabric to size. Turn in 1cm around the edges. Press. Then turn in another 1cm and stitch, leaving 8cm unstitched around each corner. *Mitre* the corners as shown on page 35. Press.

Simple chair covers

A stylish way to brighten up a plain straight-backed chair is to make a loose cover. Look for washable, shrink-resistant fabrics. You don't need much, so a bargain remnant may be suitable.

1. **Seat cover.** Measure the seat and wooden frame as shown above. Then add an extra 4cm (for hems) to each measurement. Carefully cut a piece of fabric to the required size.

Pin here

2. Place the fabric, right side down, over the seat. Make sure that it is central and that there is an extra 2cm of fabric at the back for hemming. Pin the two front corners as shown.

* It is not a good idea to join lengths of fabric for sheets as seams are uncomfortable to lie on.

Pillow cases

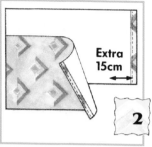

1. Measure your pillow as shown, and add 3.5cm to the length and 3cm to the width (for hems and seams). Cut one piece of fabric this size, and a second piece the same width but 15cm longer.

2. If using fabric with a directional pattern, check that the front and back pieces match. Turn in 1cm at one end of each piece of fabric. Press. Turn in 1cm more and stitch in place.

3. With right sides facing, match fabric along raw edges. Fold back the extra 15cm as shown. Pin edges together. Stitch 1.5cm and neaten*. Remove tacking and turn right way out.

Duvet covers

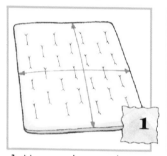

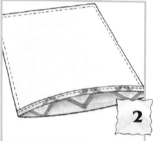

1. Measure duvet as shown. Add 3.5cm to the length and 3cm to the width (for hems and seams). If joining widths of fabric, allow an extra 1.5cm seams. Cut two pieces of fabric to size.

2. Turn in 1cm along the bottom edges of each piece of fabric. Press. Turn in 1cm more and stitch. With right sides facing, pin raw edges together. Stitch 1.5cm in and neaten*. Turn right way out.

3. Separate the two pieces of fastening tape. Pin and tack them to either side of the opening. Stitch in place. To strengthen, sew across the tape ends as shown. Remove tacking, then press.

Adding style

Decorative borders and *motifs* are a good way of adding an original finishing touch to your bed linen.

Machined borders

Many sewing machines have a range of decorative stitches which can be used to finish off edges in a contrasting colour.

Fabric borders

You can buy decorative trims such as broderie anglaise, ribbon or braid. Hand stitch them around the finished edge.

Embroidery

Embroider small motifs by hand or machine.

3. Remove the cover, then stitch along each pinned line. Trim away excess fabric and press open both seams. Turn in 1cm along each raw edge. Press. Turn in 1cm more and sew in place.

4. **Back cover.** Measure chair back as shown. Add 3.5cm to the length and 3cm to the width (for hems and seams). Cut fabric to size. Repeat with chair front, adding the same allowances.

5. With right sides facing, pin the front and back around the chair so that the seams lie along its back edges. Remove. Stitch and neaten seams. Turn in a double hem along raw edges, as before.

6. **Ties.** Use pieces of ribbon or tubes of material pressed flat. To attach ties, press both covers and put them on the chair. Pin a tie to either side of each back leg. Sew on to the back of the fabric.

---

* For maximum strength, use zig-zag stitch for neatening.

Soft furnishing accessories

Accessories, such as cushions and picture frames, add the finishing touch to a stylish room. To make them unique, you could embroider them with your own design or add an *appliquéd motif.*

Equipment checklist

- Fabric and thread
- Dressmaker's scissors
- Tape measure and pins
- Fastening tape or press studs (for cushions)
- Wall hooks and small curtain rings (for tie-backs)
- Stiff card and glue (for frame)

Cushions can be any shape or size. Large floor cushions are useful for extra seating. Smaller cushions scattered on a bed or chair make your room look cosy. Many shops sell ready-made cushion inners.

Fabric covered frames are an inexpensive way of giving your room an individual touch.

Tie-backs hold curtains in place during the day. They are attached to the wall by rings (or loops of fabric) which slip on to small wall hooks. If you don't like sewing you can still make tie-backs using ribbon or braid.

Loose cushion covers

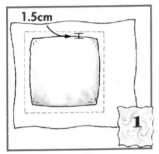

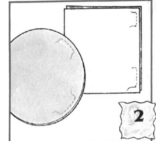

1. For round and square cushion covers, measure the cushion and add a 1.5cm seam allowance all the way round. Cut two pieces of fabric to the required size.

2. With right sides facing, mark an opening large enough for the cushion. Stitch for a few centimetres either side of it. Neaten the opening using a 1.5cm hem.

3. Pin and tack the remaining raw edges together. Stitch around the rest of the cover until you meet the smaller seams shown in step 2. Remove pins and tacking.

4. Trim seams as shown. Turn cover the right way out and sew press studs to the inside edges of the opening. Alternatively, attach fastening tape as shown on page 37.

Fabric covered frames

1. Cut two pieces of card to the size you want your frame.

2. Centre your picture on one piece of card and draw around it. Draw a line 5mm in from, and parallel to the outline. Cut along it.

3. Place fabric over the card and cut a diagonal cross over the picture area. Fold excess fabric to the back of the frame and glue in place.*

4. Cover the second piece of card with fabric, turning raw edges to the back as before.

5. Position your picture in the frame and stitch or glue the edges together.

Tie-backs

Screw in hook here.

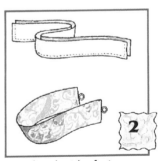

1. Estimate the length of each tie-back as shown, then decide how wide you want your ties to be. Add 1.5cm (for seams) to each measurement. Cut two pieces of fabric for each *tie-back.*

2. With right sides facing, stitch three edges together (1.5cm seam). Turn the right way out and *slipstitch* remaining edge. Sew a small curtain ring to each end of the tie.

* Trim away any excess fabric if necessary.

F looring

Interior designers often start with the floor when designing a room, then plan the furniture and *décor* around it. However, this may be impractical if you need to plan your flooring around existing décor. Some types of flooring are simple to fit yourself; others need to be fitted professionally. Below are some of the more popular ones.

In this multi-purpose room, rubber and vinyl floorings make a practical as well as an attractive combination. Coconut matting adds warmth and texture to the room on the right.

Types of flooring

Carpet. Warm, hardwearing and fairly expensive. Available in many colours, patterns and textures.

Carpet tiles. Cheaper than ordinary carpet. Easy to lay.

Vinyl. Smooth, tough surface. Comes in a range of colours and patterns.

Coconut matting. Rough surface. Hardwearing and cheap. Comes in natural colours. Easy to lay.

Cork tiles. Smooth, mottled surface. Tough and fairly cheap. Comes in natural colours. Easy to lay.

Floorboards

If your floorboards are in reasonable condition you can remove your existing flooring altogether. Sand* the boards, then cover with several coats of varnish. Alternatively, decorate them before varnishing using wood stains or eggshell paint. Apply *flat colour*, decorative paint techniques, stencils or even trompe l'oeil effects such as fake rugs or tiles (see page 33).

Practical planning

The flooring you choose should be suited to the purpose of your room or a specific area. If you have a washbasin, a waterproof surface, such as vinyl or sealed cork, is a good idea. Carpet or cork will provide good soundproofing in an exercise or rehearsal area.

For warmth and comfort underfoot, choose carpet, cork or cushioned vinyl. Alternatively, place rugs around the bed and in seating areas (this also reduces noise on hard surfaces). If you entertain a lot, carpet tiles are a good idea as they can be replaced when stained or worn.

Using pattern and colour

The way you use pattern and colour on a floor affects the proportions of your room.

★Bright, bold colours reduce space in a small room. Restrict strong colours and patterns to small areas such as rugs.

★To make a room look bigger use a plain coloured flooring and paint the skirting board to match.

★To widen a narrow room lay striped flooring widthways or lay contrasting tiles in a diamond pattern.

Rugs

Rugs are a cheap and versatile way of disguising existing flooring or hiding worn areas. They can also be used to define specific areas of your room. If your *décor* is plain, use rugs to add colour, pattern and texture. They also make hard surfaces such as vinyl more comfortable.

Flokati. Shaggy wool pile carpet. Fairly cheap.

Dhurry. Indian flat-woven rug. Fairly cheap.

Tufted rug. Similar to carpet but thicker. Wide price range.

Numdah. Small felt rug. Very cheap.

* If they are in good condition they can be sanded by hand, however an industrial sander is needed on badly stained boards.

Making simple furniture

Making your own furniture is both economical and surprisingly easy. Here, you can find out how to make a simple box-shaped unit, which can be adapted to produce a range of furniture tailored to your particular needs. There are also instructions for making a stylish and versatile screen, which can be used as a room-divider or to conceal a messy corner.

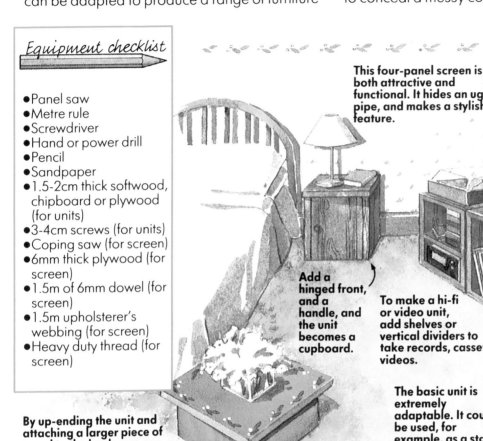

Equipment checklist

- Panel saw
- Metre rule
- Screwdriver
- Hand or power drill
- Pencil
- Sandpaper
- 1.5-2cm thick softwood, chipboard or plywood (for units)
- 3-4cm screws (for units)
- Coping saw (for screen)
- 6mm thick plywood (for screen)
- 1.5m of 6mm dowel (for screen)
- 1.5m upholsterer's webbing (for screen)
- Heavy duty thread (for screen)

This four-panel screen is both attractive and functional. It hides an ugly pipe, and makes a stylish feature.

Add a hinged front, and a handle, and the unit becomes a cupboard.

To make a hi-fi or video unit, add shelves or vertical dividers to take records, cassettes or videos.

By up-ending the unit and attaching a larger piece of wood to the back, you can transform it into a smart coffee table.

The basic unit is extremely adaptable. It could be used, for example, as a stand for a television, or to provide extra storage space.

Buying wood

Before buying wood, you need to work out how large you want your unit or screen to be. Measure the amount of space available and jot down the dimensions your furniture will need to be.

Many large stores will cut wood to the length and width you require for no extra charge.

If you are in any doubt, ask a sales assistant for advice.

Simple box unit

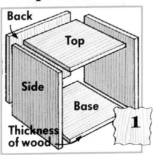

1. To make a square unit, cut four pieces of wood the same size using a panel saw. Cut a fifth piece (the back) to the same length, but add twice the thickness of the wood to the width*. Sand edges.

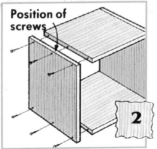

2. To attach the sides, top and base, mark the position of the screws on each piece in pencil, as shown. Drill the holes** using a hand or power drill, then screw the sides tightly into place.

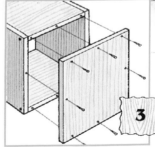

3. To attach the back, mark the position of the screws as shown above. Drill the holes, then screw the back in place. Finally, sand down any rough edges to give the unit a smooth finish.

* To make the unit taller, lengthen sides and back. To widen it, increase width of back, top and base.
   ** Make sure the holes are slightly smaller in diameter than your screws.

Practical tips

★Practise drilling and sawing on a spare piece of wood before you start.

★To get a straight line when sawing, make sure the wood is held securely. Ask a friend to help you.

★To help slide the saw through wood, rub soap on the blade.

★If cutting a *veneered* surface always score the veneer before sawing.

Unit with shelf.*

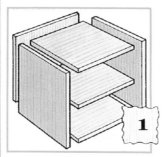

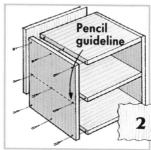

Pencil guideline

1. Using a panel saw, cut five pieces of wood to the same size (one of these pieces forms the shelf). Cut one back piece, as for the basic unit. Smooth down any rough edges with sandpaper.

2. Measure the height of the shelf on each side, and draw it in with a piece of chalk. Mark the screw positions, as shown above. Construct the unit around the shelf, as before (see left).

Finishes

Paint can be used as *flat colour* or decoratively (see page 28). Seal the surface with *primer* or *undercoat* before painting.

Clear varnish will show off the beauty of natural, bare wood.

Tinted varnish works well on wood, plywood and chipboard.

Wood stain enhances the grain of natural wood and emphasizes the interesting texture of chipboard.

A decorative collage can be protected with layers of clear varnish or, on a flat surface, with a thin sheet of glass.

Pleated or flat fabric can be attached using a staple gun. Conceal the staples with braid or a contrasting trim.

Lacquer gives a heavy duty, shiny coating to all types of surface.

Unit with vertical divider.*

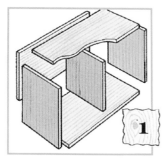

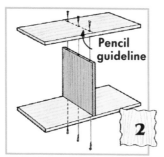

Pencil guideline

1. First cut pieces for the basic unit. To make the divider, cut out a piece of wood that is the same width as the sides, but is shorter than the height by twice the thickness of the wood.

2. Using a ruler, measure and mark the position of the divider on the top and base pieces. Mark the position of your screw holes on both, as shown. Drill the holes, then screw the pieces together.

3. Attach the sides following the instructions for constructing the basic unit (see left). Finally, screw the back into place and sand down any rough edges to give the unit a smooth finish.

Making a screen

1.8cm

Drill hole

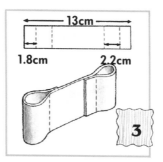

13cm

1.8cm   2.2cm

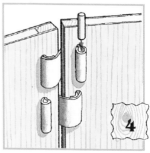

1. With a panel saw cut three plywood panels**, 1.5m high and at least 40cm wide. Mark eight slots on each panel, each one being 1.8cm from the edge, 0.6cm wide and the depth of the webbing.

2. To cut out the slots, carefully drill a hole at each end. Starting at the top of each slot, use a coping saw to cut down both sides, as shown. Smooth down the rough edges with sandpaper.

3. Cut the webbing into eight 13cm strips. On each strip, measure 1.8cm in from each end and mark. Repeat 2.2cm in from the marks. Fold over the ends to form a loop, as shown. Stitch in place.

4. Lay the panels side by side. Thread webbing through each slot. Insert a piece of dowel (same depth as webbing) in each loop to form a hinge. Finally, decorate the screen.

You can add as many shelves or dividers as you want.
**You can add more panels if you require but remember to buy extra webbing and dowels.*

Renovating furniture

Old furniture often has more style and character than modern pieces and can cost a lot less. If you know where to look, you can find a bargain which, after you have renovated it, will look as good as (or even better than) new. Start by renovating a small item, such as a chair and gradually move on to larger things as you gain confidence.

Where to look

Second-hand and junk shops make a good hunting ground, especially local ones, where you can pop in regularly to check what is available. Don't be afraid to haggle over the price – this is common practice when buying second-hand goods.

Look out for auctions, house clearances and garage sales. These may be announced from time to time in your local paper and are often worth a visit. It is best to go with the intention of buying one or two specific items, otherwise you may get carried away and come back with something irresistible but useless.

Points to remember

★Always take the measurements of your room with you when shopping for old furniture.

★Check metal items for rust. Small patches can be treated fairly easily (see right), but if there is a lot, do not buy the item. Replace rusting screws, hinges or handles.

★Remove any drawers and check the condition of the runners. Worn ones will need to be replaced.

★Loose joints and supports will need mending or strengthening.

★Tiny holes in wooden furniture are a sign of woodworm. If the problem is not too great, it can be treated with special woodworm killer and the holes filled. Do not bring woodwormy furniture into the house*.

Simple repairs

★Small holes in wood can be filled using fine wood filler. Holes in metal can be filled using **plastic padding** or metal filler. Follow the instructions on the packet for how to do it.

★You can mend loose wooden joints using wood glue.

★To treat rust, remove it using wire wool or sandpaper, then coat with metal *primer*.

★Fine scratches in wood can be filled using special tinted wax or shoe polish. Stains can be bleached out and the entire surface re-stained or painted.

Stripping surfaces

When applying a new finish to a surface, you will get a better result if you remove any paint or varnish first, with a liquid stripper. This is suitable for metal and wooden furniture, skirting boards, windows etc. Always work in a well-ventilated area, as it can be dangerous to inhale the fumes.

Equipment checklist

- Rubber gloves
- Medium-sized paint brush
- Flat scraper
- Shave hook (for carved areas)
- Liquid stripper
- Old rags
- Sandpaper
- White spirit

1. Brush on a thick coat of stripper. Leave for the recommended length of time**, then remove the paint or varnish with a scraper.

2. Apply another coat if necessary (or on stubborn areas). Wipe away all traces of stripper with warm water and a cloth. Leave to dry.

3. Smooth down the bare surface with sandpaper. Remove the dust with a dry cloth, then wipe down with white spirit. Leave to dry.

*Woodworm can easily spread to other furniture. To prevent this, keep it in a garage or outhouse.
** This is usually 5-15 minutes, but always check the instructions.

Applying a new surface

The finish on a piece of furniture provides decoration and/or protection. If a surface is poor, it will look better repainted. If it is good, a coat of varnish may be all it needs.

Using varnish

Varnish gives a tough, water-resistant surface with a shiny, satin or matt finish. Clear varnish enhances the natural colour of stripped wood. Tinted varnish will both colour and protect a surface.

Using a clean paint brush, apply a thin coat of varnish. Leave until completely dry, then apply a second coat.

Using stains

Stains come in a range of wood tones and bright colours. Use them to colour stripped wood, or to disguise repairs. Before staining, test the colour on an area which won't show. Apply with a brush or cloth along the grain of the wood. Avoid overlapping areas. Leave to dry. For added protection, add a coat of clear varnish.

Using paint

Using paint is a quick and colourful way of decorating furniture. If the surface is smooth, you can paint over existing paint. Poor quality paint and any varnish should be removed.

Apply a coat of **primer** or **undercoat** before painting with gloss or eggshell paint. For an even finish on wicker and other uneven surfaces, use spray paint.

Decorative paint effects make these functional office filing cabinets into attractive items of furniture.

Here, an old wicker chair has been given a fresh look by painting it to match the *décor*.

Stencils add interest to this brightly painted chest of drawers. They can also be used on bare wood.

Making a new cover for an old deckchair

A brightly patterned deckchair looks just as good indoors as outside.

Equipment checklist

- Heavy duty cotton or canvas
- Tape measure
- Pins
- Dressmaker's scissors
- Heavy-duty thread
- Sewing machine
- Heavy-duty machine needles
- Wood glue
- Tailor's chalk

1. Remove the cover. Measure it and add 8cm to the width and 18cm to the length. Cut your fabric to the total size.

2. Turn in a double hem 2cm deep along each long edge, pin and stitch. Turn in 1cm along each short edge, stitch.

3. For the casings, chalk a line 8cm from each short edge and fold. Stitch next to the hemmed edge. Then stitch again, 2mm in.

4. To fit, remove the wooden rods that held the old cover*. Slot them into the casings of the new one and glue rods back in place.

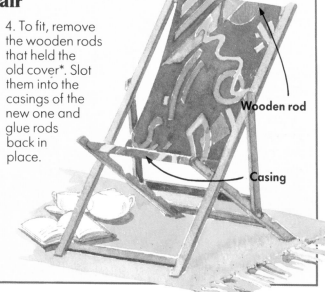

Wooden rod

Casing

*If you have difficulty, loosen the rods by tapping them gently with a mallet.

Stylish touches

Just as good clothes look incomplete without stylish accessories to set them off, your newly refurbished room will lack something without finishing touches, such as pictures, plants and favourite objects. All these things help to give it atmosphere and a sense of individuality.

You need not spend a fortune on expensive knick-knacks – it is the thought which goes into choosing and arranging accessories, rather than their cost which will set your room apart from the rest. Below are some tips, often used by professional interior designers, which will help you to get maximum impact.

Here, a cactus plant and imitation animal skin have been used to set off the safari theme of the bed and furniture.

Mass objects together to form a pleasing overall shape. Plants and pictures look good in threes and fours, rather than ones and twos.

Use objects to enhance a theme, for example, masks on the walls in an ethnic room; dried grasses, pebbles or fircones in a room with a nature theme, and so on.

Colour co-ordinate your ornaments to complement the *décor*. Striking contrasts such as black against white work very well. Another effective trick is to paint your possessions using decorative effects (you can find out how on pages 28-29).

Use contrasting textures to add visual and tactile interest to a room. Place a basket of dried flowers in front of a wrought iron fireplace, or a spiky yukka plant next to some squashy floor cushions.

Display collections attractively. Objects, such as teapots or paperweights look good set out on a well-lit shelf. Postcards, theatre programmes etc can be framed or stuck on a pin board.

The collection of shells in this thematic corner emphasizes the seaside feel of the table-top and cushion.

In this room the grey spattered typewriter and photograph frames contrast with the blue spattered desk-top.

Here, fircones, grasses and a basket of logs all contribute to the natural theme of the room.

These simple black and white objects create a pleasing outline, silhouetted against a white background.

Becoming an interior designer

Designing and decorating your own room may well have inspired you to think about taking up a career in interior design. The next three pages give you the inside information on all aspects of the job, from the qualities you will need and the mental and physical demands it makes to the rewards you can expect, in terms of pay and job satisfaction.

Do you have what it takes?

Good design and colour sense is obviously essential. However, there are other qualities that an interior designer must have in order to be a success:

★ Diplomacy, and the ability to keep calm under pressure.

★ Tolerance and flexibility; clients have been known to change their minds many times and late on in the job.

★ Numeracy and efficiency; the job involves measuring up, ordering products, dealing with tradespeople etc.

★ Objectivity; it would be wrong to impose your tastes on clients.

★ Communication skills; you will be dealing with a wide range of clients, as well as with other professionals.

★ Application; you must be ready to work hard. Early mornings on site are just as much part of the job as working at your drawing board.

Getting paid

As an interior designer, you can buy goods at wholesale prices, and will probably be able to sell them at manufacturers' recommended retail prices. Much of your profit can therefore come from the difference between the two. For some jobs, however, you are only asked to give general design advice. In this case, you need to work out in advance a fee that covers the time you will spend on a job, or fix an hourly rate.

Collecting ideas

Gather samples of fabric, wallcovering and so on from as many different sources as possible. Sketch out your ideas whenever you can; in some jobs you will be asked to design a carpet, wallcovering or fabric. It is useful to have a ready source of inspiration on hand. Keeping in contact with suppliers and manufacturers ensures that you get all the information you need on new ranges of products.

Getting there

To become an interior designer, you need both theoretical and practical knowledge.

Theory: first, take a basic course in art and design (often called a foundation course). This will develop your creative flair, colour sense etc. Then, take a professional course in interior design. You could also take evening classes in business skills, such as computing and accounting.

Practice: it is no use having good ideas if they cannot be implemented. Practical experience will help you become familiar with the different trades and craftspeople with whom you will be dealing later on. Whilst on your course, get a holiday job with an interior design or architectural practice.

orking on a job

All jobs are of course quite different, but the following example gives an insight into the order and scope of work involved in a typical interior design job.

1. The contact

Most interior design jobs begin when a client rings the interior designer's office to propose a job. They discuss the size and scope of the job, the deadline and the cost. Then, if the client and designer agree about the practical details, they arrange to meet.

2. The first meeting

The designer visits the client, usually on site, to discuss the brief (what the client wants). Sometimes a client has very definite ideas. More often, the designer has to pick up clues from the client's personality and possessions and from the building.

Here, the designer is at a fabric manufacturer's, selecting samples to show to the client.

3. Research and presentation

The designer does some research, investigating manufacturers and ranges of goods which may appeal to the client.

The next job is to draw up plans and make a sample board to help the client to visualize what the finished job could look like. Then, the interior designer shows the plans to the client and gets approval to buy materials and go ahead with the job.

Drawing up plans. The sample board shows how different colours and textures will work together.

4. Presentation

The way a designer presents his or her design influences how well or badly the client receives them. It is best to be positive and enthusiastic, but also flexible and receptive to criticism.

5. Site meeting

Any structural work is done first. The interior designer meets builders, plumbers and electricians involved with the job on site, to discuss her plans and arrange a timetable for each job.

6. Commissioning

Clients often want features specially designed for them, such as architectural mouldings or original carpets. The designer commissions the work from specialist craftspeople.

The client approves the designer's choice of curtain fabric. These colours will set the colour scheme for the room.

A meeting to discuss the layout with the builder, plumber and electrician. It is essential that everyone is briefed.

Here, a specialist plasterer makes a replica of a Georgian ceiling rose. This fits in with the style of the house.

7. Surface decoration

Once the basic structure of the house or flat is complete, the designer supervises the surface decoration. This means the coverings of the walls, floors, ceilings, woodwork and windows. It involves ordering materials and scheduling painting, laying of carpets, curtain hanging and so on, so that the work happens in the correct order, and materials do not get damaged.

The designer visits a curtain workshop to discuss the precise details of her order.

At the upholsterer's, a Queen Anne chair is being re-covered to the designer's specification.

On site, the designer supervises a curtain hanger as he fixes in place luxurious draperies.

8. Finishing touches

For some jobs, the client wants the designer to choose and install everything, down to light fittings, furniture and even cutlery.

The designer gets the client's approval before buying things and then supervises the installation and delivery of all items.

◄ A last-minute purchase by the client requires the designer to choose upholstery fabric for some dining chairs.

◄ Here, an electrician installs an ornate light fitting.

The finished ► job. The designer visits to make sure that the client is happy with the result.

Other careers

There is a wide variety of career opportunities in the world of interior design. Below are just a few of them.

In some cases, professional qualifications are essential, in others, practical skills and enthusiasm count for more. In all these careers, however, it is vital to have a flair for design and a good sense of colour.

Teacher of interior design

Description: teaching students of interior design at degree or diploma level.

Qualifications: degree or diploma in interior design, architecture or related subject. Several years' work experience in the field of design.

Personal qualities: awareness of design trends and issues. Artistic flair, patience and the ability to communicate ideas.

Getting started: build up qualifications and maintain contacts in education while acquiring work experience.

Theatre, film and television designer

Description: working, often on a freelance basis, designing and building sets for use in the theatre, film or television.

Qualifications: art school degree or diploma followed by work experience in arts or media.

Personal qualities: artistic sense and dramatic flair. Tact when dealing with people, stamina and adaptability. Good technical skills.

Getting started: enrol on a course in art or design. Then apply for a job in stage management or as an assistant in a design company or department.

Interior designer in an architectural practice

Description: working with architects on the interior of new buildings or conversions.

Qualifications: a degree or diploma in interior design or some architectural training.

Personal qualities: artistic flair and imagination. An eye for colour and detail. Good business sense and an ability to visualize end results from plans.

Getting started: apply for a place on an interior design course or enrol in a school of architecture. Try and gain practical experience in an architectural practice.

Exhibition designer

Description: designing stands and displays for exhibitions.

Qualifications: specialist courses in exhibition design are available but are not an essential requirement. Practical decorating skills and a working knowledge of carpentry would be an advantage.

Personal qualities: good communication and technical skills. Artistic sense and a good eye for detail. Energy and an ability to work under immense pressure.

Getting started: apply for a course specializing in exhibition design. Alternatively, look for a job with a company specializing in this type of work.

Furniture designer

Description: designing and producing furniture for a large manufacturing company or interior design practice. Can be employed full-time or on a freelance basis.

Qualifications: specialist training is essential. All courses involve some practical work experience.

Personal qualities: flair for colour and design. Imagination, an eye for detail and good technical skills.

Getting started: apply for a full-time or part-time course in furniture design. Then enquire about trainee posts with furniture manufacturers and cabinet makers.

Shop display designer

Description: creating window and in-store displays of merchandise in large department stores and shops. Mainly employed on a full-time basis, but some work freelance.

Qualifications: although professional qualifications are not essential, specialist training is preferred.

Personal qualities: awareness of trends, strong artistic and colour sense, good imagination and flair. Manual dexterity (the ability to work with your hands).

Getting started: enrol on a full-time course or apply for jobs in retailing which offer the opportunity of attending a day-release course.

Soft furnishings maker

Description: making up the finished product from the designer's ideas (such as curtains, bed treatments, loose covers, cushions and accessories). May work on a freelance basis or be employed by a designer, retailer or manufacturer.

Qualifications: no formal qualifications are required, although specialist courses are available.

Personal qualities: must be good with your hands and have basic sewing skills. An understanding of textiles and an ability to work from rough designs.

Getting started: enrol on a course and gain as much work experience as possible. Try to get a job in a large workroom. Apply for related courses, such as upholstery, to expand your areas of expertise.

Product designer and colourist

Description: designing new ranges of textiles, wallpapers or ceramics and choosing the various colour combinations. Usually works within the design department of a large manufacturer, but can work on a freelance basis.

Qualifications: a basic design qualification is essential. An advanced specialist course would also be useful.

Personal qualities: exceptional colour sense and artistic flair. Good imagination and an ability to communicate your ideas to others. Some scientific knowledge.

Getting started: apply for a place on a design course which specializes in your chosen area (for example textile design). Gain work experience in a manufacturing company.

Commercial interior designer

Description: designing interiors for hotels, shops and restaurants and so on. Designers may be employed full-time by a retailing or catering chain or by an interior design company specializing in this type of work. Alternatively, they may work on freelance basis.

Qualifications: a degree or diploma in interior design is desirable, however this is not essential.

Personal qualities: good imagination and artistic sense. An eye for detail and an understanding of business are also important.

Getting started: apply for a course in interior design. Enquire about trainee posts and junior positions in a design company or the design department of a large organization.

Painter and decorator

Description: carrying out the practical work of painting and decorating. Many decorators work on a freelance basis; others are employed by a building or decorating firm.

Qualifications: none essential, however a basic decorating qualification would be an advantage.

Personal qualities: practical skills, dexterity, fitness and attention to detail.

Getting started: enrol on a full-time course or enquire about night classes. Ask about trainee posts with a large building or decorating company or apply for a job as an assistant with an independent decorator.

Colour consultant

Description: advising manufacturers on colours and colour ranges of paint, tiles, flooring and so on. Consultants may work on a freelance basis or be employed full-time by a large company.

Qualifications: a degree or diploma in design. Some experience in retailing, marketing or market research would be useful.

Personal qualities: exceptional colour sense and artistic flair. The ability to get on with people. Some scientific knowledge.

Getting started: apply for a place on a design course. To gain practical experience, try getting a part-time job in retailing or manufacturing.

Specialist painter

Description: carrying out specialist decorative work (for example, stencils and murals) for private clients.

Qualifications: none essential, however a professional qualification is desirable.

Personal qualities: tact when dealing with people and the ability to communicate design ideas. Some technical skills and an awareness of trends.

Getting started: enrol on a course in art or design. Enquire about trainee posts with large design companies or established painters. Whenever possible, take advanced courses to keep an eye on changing trends and techniques.

Murals to copy

Stencils to copy

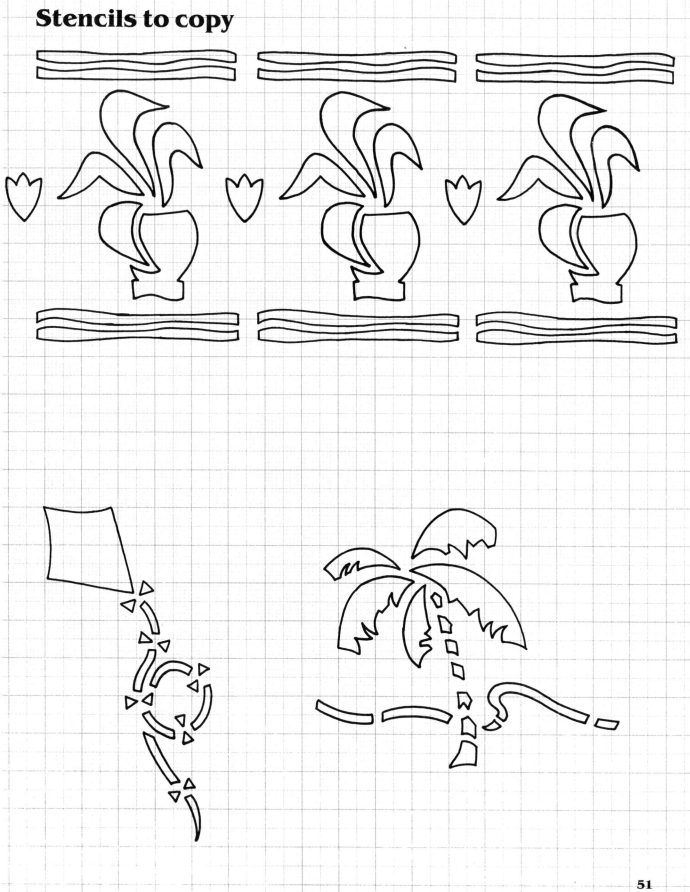

Preparing surfaces

Surface	Preparation
Paint	Poorly applied paint needs removing (see below). An even surface can be cleaned with sugar soap or detergent, then sanded smooth.
Wallpaper	Remove if hanging new paper (see below). To paint, wipe down with sugar soap or mild detergent.
Powdery plaster	Apply a coat of stabilizing solution. This is brushed on and holds the plaster together.
New plaster	Wipe down to remove any dust. If painting, prime with diluted emulsion paint. If wallpapering, prime with size (this seals the surface).
Mould	Remove with a fungicidal wash; or soak with diluted bleach, leave for 48 hours and wash off. Use fungicidal paint or paste.
Flaking paint	Remove flakes with scraper. Sand smooth.
Small cracks/holes in plaster	Remove dust and dampen area to be filled. Apply all-purpose filler. Sand smooth when dry.
Large holes in plaster	In solid walls, fill with plaster. In plasterboard cover the hole with sealing tape, then apply a thin layer of filler.
Cracks in paint	Small areas can be rubbed down with wet and dry paper (see page 58). Large areas need removing (see below).
Cracks/holes in wood	Apply flexible multi-purpose or wood filler. Use a tinted wood filler if leaving wood bare.

Stripping surfaces

Wallpaper. Turn off electricity supply. Score the wallpaper then soak with water and leave for 15mins. Starting at a seam, remove paper with a broad-bladed scraper. Repeat if necessary. Waterproof or painted paper may need steam stripping – a suitable tool may be hired.

Large areas of paint. The quickest method is to burn it off.* Use a blow torch or hot air gun to soften the paint. Scrape away the paint with a flat scraper or shave hook (for mouldings).

Paint and varnish. Chemical strippers are particularly useful for removing paint or varnish from intricate woodwork or mouldings. You can find out how to use them on page 42.

Wood

Type	Description	Uses
Hardwood (e.g. oak, beech)	Any wood from deciduous trees.	Furniture, doors, shelves
Softwood (e.g. pine, cedar)	Any wood from coniferous trees.	Shelves, furniture, doors
Hardboard	Wood dust compressed and bonded. Has tough shiny finish on one side and a textured finish on the other.	Backing for cupboards, units and so on. Also used as dividers. Covers uneven floors and surfaces.
Chipboard	Wood chips bonded together to form a coarse-grained board.	Shelves, units, tables and cupboards. Covering uneven floors.
Plywood	Thin sheets of wood glued together.	Shelves, units, screens.
Melamine	Laminated (plastic-coated) chipboard.	Shelves, tables, units, wardrobes, cupboards
Medium-density fibreboard (MDF)	Wood fibres bonded together to give a fine, even textured surface.	Shelves, tables, units, cupboards

Finishes

Type	Appearance	Application
Varnish	Matt, satin or gloss finish.	Apply with a brush in thin layers.
Stain	Natural finish that colours wood without hiding the grain.	Apply one even coat with a brush or rag.
Wax	Soft, satin finish.	Apply with a rag in several thin layers. Then buff with a soft cloth.
Oil (teak, linseed)	A natural finish that enhances the grain and may darken the wood.	Apply with a rag in thin layers.

This can be dangerous. It is best to ask someone experienced at using a blow torch to help you.

Paint

Cost	Comments
Ranges from fairly expensive to very expensive.	Very strong. Can be painted, varnished, waxed, oiled or stained.
Fairly cheap	Not as durable as hardwood. Can be painted, varnished, waxed, stained, oiled.
Very cheap	Lightweight and not very strong. Usually left untreated. Can be painted or stained.
Cheap	Also comes with wood or plastic veneer. Weaker than wood. Can be painted, varnished or stained.
Cheap to fairly expensive	Fairly strong. Also comes with wood or plastic veneer. Non-veneered plywood can be painted, varnished or stained.
Fairly cheap	Comes in many colours. May split or chip.
Fairly cheap	Easy to cut and shape. Must be painted or varnished.

Type	Uses	Solvent/ thinner	Drying time	Comments
Primer (all-purpose, wood, metal)	Seals all types of bare surface ready for painting.	White spirit	8-12 hrs	Cannot be used as a topcoat.
Undercoat	Basecoat for gloss or eggshell.	White spirit	8-12 hrs	Cannot be used as a topcoat. Prevents old colour showing through.
Emulsion (liquid or solid)	Water-based paint for walls and ceilings. Matt or silk finishes available.	Water	4 hrs	Shows scuff marks. Silk emulsion highlights uneven surfaces.
Eggshell	Oil-based paint. Produces a tough, washable, matt surface on walls, wood and metal.	White spirit	12-16 hrs	Easier to apply than gloss paint.
Gloss (liquid or non-drip)	Oil-based paint. Produces a tough, washable, shiny surface on walls, wood and metal.	White spirit	12-16 hrs	Highlights flaws, so ensure surface is even. Liquid gloss is harder to apply.
Textured paint	Gives a rough, textured finish to walls and ceilings.	Water	12-16 hrs	Hard to clean and difficult to remove. Disguises uneven surfaces.
Acrylic	Brightly coloured water-based paint used in stencilling and murals.	Water	Within minutes	Expensive if used over large areas. Can deepen colour by applying several layers.
Stencilling crayons	Sticks of solid oil-based paint.	White spirit	Dries immediately	Easy to use and almost smudge-free.

Comments
Clear and tinted varnishes available. Hardwearing and water-resistant.
Colours range from wood tones to bright primary colours. Coat with clear varnish for added protection. Subsequent coats darken the colour.
Clear and tinted waxes available.
Teak finish is moderately heat- and water-resistant. Linseed is not so durable. Surface will need re-oiling from time-to-time.

Estimating quantities

You can find out how much paint you need by referring to the chart below. To estimate the area to be covered, measure the height of your wall and the distance around the walls (including windows and doors), then multiply the two measurements together.

Paint	Quantity	Area covered
Primer	1 litre	7-8m² (wood) 9-11m² (metal) 5-9m² (plaster)
Undercoat	1 litre	15m²
Emulsion	1 litre	14-15m²
Eggshell	1 litre	15m²
Liquid gloss	1 litre	17m²
Non-drip gloss	1 litre	12m²

Wallpaper

Wallpaper	Description	Recommended adhesive*	Method of hanging	Cost	Comments
Standard	Flat printed or slightly textured paper, available in a wide range of colours and patterns.	Regular, ready-mixed or all-purpose paste. Also available ready-pasted.	Paste paper. If ready-pasted, immerse lengths into trough of water.	Wide price range	Do not use near moisture (eg. around a basin) as it absorbs water.
Lining	Fine, flat unprinted paper, usually white or cream.	All-purpose paste	Paste paper	Cheap	Used to level out uneven walls before hanging decorative paper or painting.
Vinyl	PVC layer, paper backed, in a range of patterns and colours and a variety of textures. May be embossed.	Vinyl paste or a fungicidal, ready-mixed or all-purpose paste. Also available ready-pasted.	Paste paper backing. If ready-pasted, immerse lengths in trough of water.	Wide price range	Hardwearing, water-resistant and washable. Easy to hang. When stripped, leaves paper backing on wall.
Washable	Same as standard paper, but with a waterproof coating which can be matt or shiny.	All-purpose or ready-mixed paste	Paste paper	Fairly expensive	Be careful when sponging as tends to scuff. Difficult to remove.
Foamed polyethylene	Lightweight paper with a matt finish. Warm to the touch.	Heavy-duty or all-purpose paste.	Paste the wall.	Fairly cheap	Simple to hang. Easy to strip.
Embossed	White paper with a textured or raised pattern, which creates a 3-D effect.	Heavy-duty, ready-mixed or all-purpose paste.	Paste paper and leave to soak in before hanging. Do not use a seam roller or press against pattern when hanging.	Fairly cheap to expensive.	Needs painting. Ideal for disguising uneven surfaces. Difficult to hang on ceilings as it is fairly heavy.
Woodchip	White wallpaper with chips of wood in it which create a textured surface.	All-purpose or ready-mixed paste.	Paste paper. Do not use a seam roller.	Cheap	Needs to be painted. Easy to hang and useful for disguising uneven surfaces.
Cork	Cork backed with paper. Has a warm, textured surface.	Heavy-duty, all-purpose or ready-mixed paste.	Paste the wall.	Expensive	Difficult to hang and wears fairly quickly. Good insulator.
Hessian	Hessian backed with paper or latex. Also unbacked.	Heavy-duty or all-purpose paste.	Paste paper backing. Paste wall for unbacked.	Fairly expensive Unbacked is cheaper.	Avoid getting paste on surface. Only attempt if you have experience.
Metallic	Foil backed with paper. Shiny, surface. Usually printed with bold patterns.	Fungicidal paste.	Paste the wall or paper backing.	Expensive	Difficult to hang. Only use on an even surface and keep away from electrical fittings. Washable.

Estimating quantities

1. Check the length of one roll of wallpaper and the depth of any *pattern repeat* (see below). Measure the height of your room from the skirting board and add the pattern repeat to this measurement.

   This will give you the *drop.* Now divide the length of the roll by the drop and round the figure you get down to the nearest whole number (A).

2. Measure the distance around the room including doors and windows. Divide that figure by the width of the wallpaper. Round up the figure you get to the nearest whole number (B).

3. Divide B by A and round up the figure you get to the nearest whole number to give you the number of rolls to buy.

Pattern matching

When buying wallpaper with a directional pattern, matching consecutive sheets will waste some paper because the top of the wall rarely coincides with the point where a new pattern sequence begins. The maximum wastage to allow for each sheet is the depth of one *pattern repeat.* For example, if the pattern repeat is 25cm deep and your room 3m high, you will need 3.25m for each length.

* You can find out more about adhesives on page 58.

International wallpaper symbols

〜 Spongeable

≋ Washable

≋ Superwashable

▅ Scrubbable

☀ May fade slightly

☼ Does not fade

Strippable

Peelable

Ready-pasted

Paste the wall

Non-matching

Straight match

Offset match

$\frac{50}{25}$ cm Design repeat, distance offset

Co-ordinated fabric available

↑ Direction of hanging

↑↓ Reverse alternate lengths

Embossed

Batch numbers

Wallpaper is printed in batches. Each roll within a batch carries the same number. When buying wallpaper, pick rolls with the same number, as colour can vary between different batches.

If you are unsure about the exact quantity you require, ask the assistant to put an extra roll from the same batch on one side for you.

Flooring

Type	Description	Ease of laying	Cost	Comments
Carpet (woven, tufted and non-woven)	Usually pure wool or a mixture of wool and synthetic fibres, on a foam or hessian backing. Wide range of patterns, colours and textures.	Best fitted professionally.	Wide price range	Needs underlay. Comfortable, quiet and warm underfoot. Cheap carpet tends to scuff.
Carpet tiles	Squares of carpet on a durable backing. Available in plain colours and some patterns.	Very easy	Cheap to expensive.	Can be moved around easily and squares can be replaced when stained or worn.
Cork tiles	Squares of cork. Limited range of colours.	Fairly easy. Protect with varnish.	Fairly cheap.	Warm underfoot. Good sound-proofer. Wears well. Ready-sealed tiles do not need varnishing but are more expensive.
Vinyl	Smooth, water-resistant surface. Wide range of colours and patterns.	Best fitted professionally.	Fairly cheap to expensive.	Hardwearing. Cool underfoot. Poor sound-proofer. Slippery when wet.
Cushioned vinyl	Vinyl with a foam and fibre-glass backing. Textured surface.	Best fitted professionally.	Fairly cheap to expensive.	Comfortable, warm and quiet underfoot.
Vinyl tiles	Squares of standard or cushioned vinyl.	Easy, especially if tiles are self-adhesive.	Fairly cheap. Cushioned vinyl tiles are slightly more expensive.	Flexible and hardwearing.
Rubber	Mixture of natural and synthetic rubbers. May have raised studs, ribs or squares.	Best fitted professionally.	Fairly cheap to expensive	Hardwearing and fairly quiet underfoot. Surface tends to mark easily. Raised surfaces tend to collect dirt.
Rubber tiles	Squares of rubber in a wide range of colours. Can also get marbled and stone effects.	Fairly easy	Fairly expensive	Flexible and hardwearing.
Linoleum	Smooth, water-resistant surface. Comes in a wide range of marbled colours.	Fairly difficult. Best fitted professionally.	Fairly cheap to quite expensive.	Very tough. Cold underfoot. Can be cut into intricate patterns and shapes. Also available as tiles.
Vegetable matting (coconut, sisal, coir)	Rough, textured matting made from vegetable fibres. Comes in strips and squares. Limited colour range.	Easy	Fairly cheap	Very hardwearing. Rough underfoot. Tends to collect dust.
Wood	Exposed floorboards. Limited colour choice.	New boards must be laid professionally. Old boards need sanding smooth and any gaps filled.	Cheap if restoring old boards. Expensive if fitting new boards.	Extremely hardwearing. Fairly warm but poor for soundproofing. Can be varnished, stained or painted.

Fabric

Fabric	Description	Suitability	Cost	Comments
Acrylic	Soft, lightweight man-made fibre. Can look like wool.	Bed covers, curtains, cushions, table-cloths and upholstery.	Quite cheap to quite expensive.	Warm, strong and crease-resistant. Dries very quickly.
Calico	Light to mediumweight, coarse cotton fabric. Dull finish in natural colours.	Blinds. Also used as a base cover for sofas and chairs.	Cheap	Washes and wears well. Tends to crease.
Canvas	A strong, stiff heavy fabric made from coarse cotton, linen or synthetic fibres.	Deck chairs, director's chairs and floor covering.	Fairly expensive	Must be sewn with heavy duty needle and thread.
Chintz	Plain or printed cotton with a glazed (shiny) finish.	Curtains, loose covers and upholstery.	Fairly cheap to expensive.	Not very hardwearing. Crease- and dirt-resistant.
Cotton	Comes in a wide range of weights and finishes.	Bed linen, curtains, blinds, cushions, loose covers, table-cloths and upholstery.	Wide price range	Tends to crease easily. A cotton synthetic mixture may be a better idea.
Felt	Smooth, mediumweight, non-woven fabric made by pressing fibres together.	Mainly used to cover pinboards. Good wall or temporary floor covering.	Fairly cheap	Does not fray. Cannot be washed. Can buy window dresser's felt which is more hardwearing.
Hessian	A strong, heavyweight, rough fabric made from jute or hemp. Comes in natural colours and a limited range of dyed colours.	Upholstery, wallcovering, curtains and blinds.	Cheap	Hard to keep clean and coarse to the touch. Frays very easily.
Lace	Very light, open-work fabric made from cotton, viscose or nylon.	Curtains, blinds, bedspreads and table-cloths.	Fairly expensive	See-through lace curtains on their own do not provide privacy.
Linen	Mediumweight fabric woven from flax. It has a slightly textured appearance.	Bedcovers, loose covers, curtains, blinds, cushions, serviettes and table-cloths.	Expensive	Very strong. Creases easily and tends to shrink. Better if mixed with other fibres e.g cotton.
Muslin	Lightweight gauze made from cotton.	Lightweight curtains	Cheap	Can buy stiffened muslin. Tends to shrink and crease.
Net	Very light, open-mesh, almost transparent fabric made from cotton, silk or man-made fibres. Usually white or cream.	Mainly used for curtains.	Cheap	Does not fray when cut so no need to neaten. Tends to yellow with age. Easy to dye.
Polyester	Lightweight, man-made fibre which can look like wool, silk or cotton.	Bedcovers, curtains, blinds, cushions and table-cloths.	Fairly cheap	Often mixed with natural fibres. Easy to clean and does not crease.
Poplin	Light to mediumweight cotton or rayon fabric which has a fine rib and slight sheen.	Curtains, blinds and loose covers.	Fairly cheap	Drapes well. Choose heavier, ribbed fabric for loose covers.
Wool	Warm, soft, mediumweight fabric. Comes in many different textures.	Bedcovers, curtains, cushions, table covers and upholstery.	Expensive	Very tough but has a tendency to shrink. Also comes mixed with synthetic fibres.

Estimating fabric quantities for curtains

1. Measure the length of your curtain track or pole.

2. Decide where you want your curtains to come down to and measure the distance between that point and the track or pole.

3. To calculate the width of your curtains multiply the track/pole length by your required fabric fullness.

This depends on your heading tape – there are several different kinds to choose from (see opposite).

4. Divide this number by the width of fabric you want to use* (round it up to the nearest full number). Then multiply it by the length of your curtains. Add 20cm for each fabric width to give the right quantity to buy.

56   *Fabric is sold in standard widths.*

Pattern matching

If you are using a patterned fabric, add the length of one *pattern repeat* (see page 54) per fabric width, to your final figure.

Heading tape

Standard. For lightweight curtains under a pelmet/valance. Fabric fullness — 1·5-2 x track length.

Pencil pleat. For all types of curtains on tracks or poles. Fabric fullness — 2.25 x track/pole length

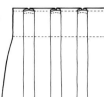

Box pleats. For most types of curtains on tracks and poles. Fabric fullness — 2 x track/pole length.

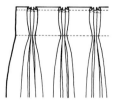

Triple pleats. Good for formal curtains on tracks or poles. Fabric fullness — 2 x track/pole length.

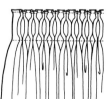

Smocked. For most types of curtains on tracks and poles. Fabric fullness — 2 x track/pole length.

Ties. For light- or mediumweight curtains on poles. Fabric fullness — 2 x pole length

Loops. For all types of curtains on poles. Fabric fullness — 1 pole length plus side hem allowances.

Fixtures and fittings

Shelving

It is important to mark out accurately the position of your shelves. Always use a metre rule (a fabric tape measure may stretch). Once in place use a spirit level to check that the shelving is straight.

Fixture	Mounting	Cost	Comments
Alcove shelving	Screw wooden battens to wall, at either end of shelf. Place shelf on top.	Very cheap	Simple to make and quite sturdy.
Brackets	Screw long arm to wall and short arm to shelf. Shelf should not overhang brackets by more than 2.5cm.	Fairly cheap	Supports heavy loads. Brackets can be plain or decorative, e.g. ornate iron work.
Open tracks	Screw tracks to wall and shelves to brackets. Attach brackets. Shelf should not overhang brackets by more than 2.5cm.	Range from fairly cheap to expensive.	Can take medium to heavy loads. Come in a wide variety of colours. Flexible, as height of shelves can be adjusted.
Bookcase tracks	Screw tracks into wall, at either end of shelf. Screw support clips to shelf. Attach clips to tracks.	Fairly cheap to expensive.	Flexible as height of shelves can be adjusted. Takes fairly light loads, tends to bow under heavy loads.
Pegs	Wooden or plastic pegs are screwed to wall or fixed into ready-made holes, at either end of shelf.	Very cheap	Can only be used for very light loads. Good for display cabinets.
Cantilever	U-shaped attachment is screwed to wall. The shelf then slots into it.	Fairly cheap	Takes very light loads only. Extremely neat finish, but not as flexible as many other systems.

Curtain tracks and poles

Net track. Thin rigid track for hanging net or café curtains. You can buy extendible track or specific lengths.

Curtain wire. Length of wire for hanging net or café curtains. Attached to window frame with small hooks.

Plastic and metal tracks. Rigid track is suitable for straight windows, flexible track for straight or bay windows. Functional rather than decorative. Come in standard lengths that can be trimmed at home, or extendible lengths. Attached to the wall with special fitting provided.

Poles. Suitable for straight windows. Decorative as well as functional feature. You can buy brass or wooden poles in standard lengths. Extendible metal poles are also available. Attached to the wall with brackets supplied.

Curved poles and tracks. For bay windows. Bought made-to-measure, so more costly than straight track or poles.

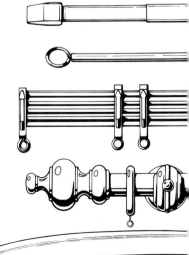

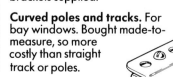

Equipment

Item	Uses	Cost	What to look for	Comments
Paste brush	Large brush for applying paste to wallpaper or walls.	Fairly cheap	Choose a good quality brush that does not shed bristles.	You will need to buy a suitable size and shape of brush for the job in hand. Make sure you clean all brushes properly after use, or they may rot. To protect the bristles wrap them in newspaper or clingfilm and do not crush them in storage, as they will not regain their shape.
Wallpapering brush	Soft-bristled brush for smoothing out wallpaper when hung.	Fairly cheap	Ensure handle is wide enough to grip comfortably. Bristles should have soft, rounded ends.	
Paint brushes (2.5-10cm)	Applying paint to walls and woodwork.	Prices vary	Bristles should be straight, not splayed. Should not shed.	
Cutting-in brush	Angled brush for applying paint to window frames and surface edges.	Fairly cheap	Check that bristles form an even, flat angle.	
Artist's brush	Fine brush for detailed work and outlines.	Fairly expensive	Buy a sable brush. Make sure hairs form a fine tip.	
Stencil brush	Applying paint to walls through a stencil.	Fairly expensive	Bristles should be stiff and bushy.	
Roller and tray	Applying emulsion paint to large flat areas, such as walls and ceilings.	Fairly cheap	Choose a sheepskin roller rather than a foam one. Make sure it has a thick pile. Check that the tray is sturdy and fits the roller.	Remove all traces of paint from the roller and tray. Store roller on its end. You can also buy textured rollers which trace a pattern in the paint.
Crevice (radiator) roller	Long handle enables you to reach behind radiators and into crevices.	Fairly cheap		
Flat scraper	Has broad blade for stripping wallpaper or paint from flat surfaces.	Fairly cheap	Check for flexibility by gently pressing down on tip of scraper.	Once cleaned, make sure the blade is thoroughly dry or it may rust. Lightly oil before storing.
Shave hook	Triangular blade for stripping paint or varnish from carved or moulded surfaces.	Fairly cheap	Make sure the edges are not too sharp.	
Wallpapering scissors	Long blades for scoring, trimming and cutting wallpaper.	Fairly cheap to quite expensive.	Check blades align correctly, are rust-free and sharp.	It is worth spending the money on a pair of good quality scissors, as these will last longer than a poor quality pair.
Dress-maker's scissors	For cutting fabric.	Fairly expensive		
Pinking shears	Scissors with serrated blades for neatening fabric.	Fairly expensive		
Trimming knife	Trimming, scoring and cutting paper, card, carpet, tiles and wallpaper.	Plastic cased knives are fairly cheap. Metal ones are more expensive.	For safety, buy a knife that has a retractable blade.	Clean after use and dry thoroughly to avoid rusting. Make sure the blade is covered when storing.
Craft knife	Small knife for cutting and scoring acetate, card and paper.	Cheap	Buy one with a detachable blade, so that it can be changed when blunt.	

Abrasive papers

Sandpaper (or glasspaper). This is made in different grades of roughness and is mainly used to smooth surfaces. Rough paper removes coarse surfaces. Fine paper is used to give a smooth finish.

Wet and dry paper. This is used with water or a solvent depending on the surface.

Adhesives

Powdered wallpaper paste. Sticks ordinary lightweight paper. Mix with water.

Fungicidal wallpaper paste. Prevents mould forming. Used on non-porous paper such as vinyl.

Ready-mixed wallpaper paste. Comes in a tub ready to use. Can contain a fungicide.

All-purpose wallpaper paste. Can be used on any type of wallcovering. Can be bought as a powder or ready-mixed.

Heavy-duty wallpaper paste. Used for hanging heavy paper, such as embossed paper or paper-backed fabrics.

Wood glue. Sticks all types of lightweight wood.

Resin wood glue. Waterproof bond for all types of wood.

Contact adhesive. Sticks veneer or laminate to board.

Resin glue. Waterproof bond for almost any surface.

Drill bits

Attachments for electric and hand drills which make the holes. Come in a range of sizes.

Twist bit. Makes ordinary holes to take the screw.

Countersunk bit. Makes an additional shallow hole to take the head of a countersunk screw so that it sits flush with the surface.

Item	Uses	Cost	What to look for	Comments
Panel saw	All-purpose saw. Good for cutting large pieces of timber such as planks.	Expensive	Test blade for sharpness and handle for comfort. Check teeth — the more teeth the blade has, the finer and slower the cut. Hard-tipped saws are best, as they do not require sharpening.	Oil blade lightly after use to prevent rusting. To store, hang saw up by the handle and protect the blade with a saw guard.
Tenon saw	All-purpose saw. Good for smaller pieces of wood and accurate work.	Fairly expensive		
Coping saw	Adjustable blade, for sawing small areas and awkward shapes.	Fairly cheap		
Cross-slot screwdriver	Unscrewing and screwing in cross-slot screws.	Fairly cheap	Make sure handle is the right length in proportion to the blade. If it is too short you will not be able to twist it easily.	Both left-handed and right-handed screwdrivers are available. Always clean handle after use. Come in various sizes.
One-slot screwdriver	Unscrewing and screwing in single-slot screws.	Fairly cheap		
Warrington pattern hammer	All-purpose hammer.	Cheap to expensive.	A wooden handle is more comfortable to hold than a steel handle with a plastic grip.	To keep the hammer head smooth and clean, rub it with fine glass paper.
Pin hammer	Lightweight hammer for panel pins and small nails.	Fairly cheap		
Claw hammer	For larger jobs, e.g floorboards. Use the claw to pull out nails.	Cheap to expensive .		
Wooden mallet	For jobs requiring less force than a hammer exerts, or where a metal head might cause damage.	Fairly cheap to expensive.	A rubber-tipped mallet will not mark wood.	Mallets can also be used to knock handles of tools e.g., when chiselling.
Electric drill	Making holes. Useful for drilling thick or hard materials.	Expensive	Look for a drill with more than one speed setting.	Both take twist and countersunk drill bits which are bought separately. Electric drills can be hired.
Hand drill	Making holes up to 8mm in diameter.	Fairly expensive	Test grip and ease of handling.	
Staple gun	Industrial stapler for rapid fixing of chair covers, wall coverings and so on.	Fairly expensive	One which takes fairly heavy staples. Otherwise may not be strong enough to hold fabric/paper.	Keep clean and dust-free.
Spirit level	Finding true vertical and horizontal lines. Ensuring surfaces are level.	Fairly cheap. Metal and wooden ones cost more than plastic.	Choose one that is clearly marked for easy reading.	
Plumb bob	Weight on long cord for marking out straight vertical lines.	Cheap	Look for a brightly coloured or metal one that stands out against the wall.	You can make your own by attaching a small weight to a piece of string.
Seam roller	Small roller for securing and smoothing down seams and joins in wallpaper and flattening borders.	Cheap	Good handle grip and flexible roller.	Do not use a seam roller on embossed paper.

Nails

Round wire nail. Strong nail for general purpose work.

Oval wire nail. Nail with oval head. It is less likely to split wood.

Panel pin. Fine nail for plywood and hardboard.

Masonry nail. Very strong nail for walls.

Floorboard nail. Rectangular nail that does not split wood.

Clout. Large nail with flat head for felt or canvas.

Chair nail. Copper, chrome or bronze nail with rounded head. Used for upholstery.

Tack. Stout angular nail, with flat head. For fixing furniture covers and carpets.

Screws

Countersunk head. Head fits flush with surface. Come with one-slot or cross-slot heads.

Raised head. Only half the head fits into surface. Come with one-slot or cross-slot heads.

Chipboard screw. Has a long thread for extra grip. Single slot head only.

Wallplugs

Wallplugs are used to help screws grip in masonry. The plug is pushed into the drill hole and the screw is screwed into it.

Fibre plug. Made from compressed fibres. Gives a strong grip in most types of solid wall.

Plastic wallplug. Split at the base so that it expands to fit the drill hole when the screw is screwed into it. Suitable for solid walls.

Hooked wallplug. Has hooks attached to the outside so that it grips the wall and cannot be pulled out. Good for heavy loads and cavity walls.

Going further

If you would like to find out more about interior design, the selected books and courses listed on these two pages, will give you a good starting point.

Book list

Better Lighting
Jeremy Myerson
Conran Octopus Ltd

Carpentry
Alec Limon & Paul Curtis
Octopus Books Ltd*

Chairs, Cushions & Coverings
Lorrie Mack
Conran Octopus Ltd*

Choosing a Colour Scheme
Ward Lock Ltd
(Not available in USA)

Conran Directory of Design
S Boyley
Conran Octopus Ltd*

Creative Home Decorating
Ward Lock Ltd
(Not available in USA)

Creative Ideas with Colour
Ward Lock Ltd
(Not available in USA)

Curtains & Blinds
Caroline Clifton-Mogg
Conran Octopus Ltd
(Publishers in USA: Random House;
Canada: General Publishing;
Australia: Angus & Robertson; New
Zealand: Octopus)

Curtains & Soft Furnishings
Ward Lock Ltd

Decorators' Directory of Style
Jocasta Innes
W. H. Smith
(Publishers in USA: Gallery; Canada:
B. Mitchell; Australia and New
Zealand: Golden Press)

Fabric Magic
Melanie Paine
Francis Lincoln
(Publishers in USA and Canada:
Pantheon; Australia and New
Zealand: Collins)

Floors & Flooring
Jane Lott
Conran Octopus Ltd*

How to Restore and Repair
Practically Everything
Lorraine Johnson
McGraw-Hill Book Company
(Publishers in USA, Australia and
New Zealand: Viking Penguin;
Canada: Fitzhenry & Whiteside)

Living in Small Spaces
Lorrie Mack
Conran Octopus Ltd**

Low Cost High Style
Elizabeth Wilhide & Andrea Spencer
Conran Octopus Ltd**

Mary Gilliat's New Guide to
Decorating
Mary Gilliat
Conran Octopus Ltd**

Paint Magic (revised edition)
Jocasta Innes
Francis Lincoln
(Publishers in USA and Canada:
Pantheon; Australia and New
Zealand: Doubleday)

Paint Techniques
Andrea Spencer
Conran Octopus Ltd*

Storage Solutions
Gilly Love
Conran Octopus Ltd*

The Conran Beginner's Guide to
Decorating
Jocasta Innes & Jill Blake
Conran Octopus Ltd
(Publishers in USA: Viking; Canada:
General Publishing; Australia: Angus
& Robertson; New Zealand: Octopus)

The Decorated Room
Lorraine Johnson & Gabrielle
Townsend
Webb & Bower (Publishers) Ltd
(Publishers in USA and Canada:
Overlook Press; Australia and New
Zealand: Penguin)

The Soft Furnishing Book
Terence Conran
Conran Octopus Ltd**

The Stencil Book
Amelia Saint George
Conran Octopus Ltd*

Courses
UK courses

Aberdeen College of Commerce
Holburn Street
Aberdeen AB9 2YT

Offers: Higher National Certificate in
Spatial Design.

**Bournemouth and Poole College of Art and
Design**
Wallisdown Road
Poole BH12 5HH

Offers: B/TEC National Diploma in Design

Bradford and Ilkley Community College
Great Horton Road
Bradford BD7 1AY

Offers: B/TEC National Diploma in Design

Brighton Polytechnic
Grand Parade
Brighton BN2 2JY

Offers: BA (Hons) in Three-dimensional
Design

**Buckinghamshire College of Higher
Education**
Queen Alexandra Road
High Wycombe HP11 2JZ

Offers: BA (Hons) in Interior Design

Chelsea School of Art
Lime Grove
London W12 8EB

Offers: College Certificate in Interior
Decoration; B/TEC Higher National
Diploma in Design

Chesterfield College of Technology and Arts
Infirmary Road
Chesterfield S41 7NG

Offers: B/TEC National Diploma in Three-
dimensional Design Studies

City College (Liverpool)
Myrtle Street
Liverpool L7 7HE

Offers: B/TEC National Diploma in Interior
Design

Dewsbury College
Cambridge Street
Batley WF17 5JB

Offers: B/TEC National Diploma in
Design; B/TEC Higher National Diploma
in Design

*Publishers in USA: Villard; Canada: General Publishing; Australia: Angus & Robertson; NZ: Octopus.
**Publishers in USA: Little Brown; Canada, Australia and New Zealand as above.

Duncan of Jordanstone College of Art
Perth Road
Dundee DD1 4HT

Offers: BA in Interior Design; BA (Hons) in Interior Design; Postgraduate Diploma in Interior Design

Edinburgh College of Art
Lauriston Place
Edinburgh EH3 9DF

Offers: BA (Hons) in Interior Design; Postgraduate Diploma in Interior Design; Master of Design in Interior Design

Glasgow School of Art
167 Renfrew Street
Glasgow G3 6RQ

Offers: BA in Interior Design; BA (Hons) in Interior Design; Postgraduate Diploma in Interior Design

Inchbald School of Design
7 Eaton Gate
London SW1W 9BA

Offers: College Diploma in Interior Design

Jacob Kramer College
Vernon Street
Leeds LS2 8PH

Offers: B/TEC National Diploma in Design

Kingston Polytechnic
Knights Park
Kingston-upon-Thames KT1 2QJ

Offers: BA (Hons) in Interior Design

Leeds Polytechnic
Calverley Street
Leeds LS1 3HE

Offers: BA (Hons) in Three-dimensional Design

Leicester Polytechnic
PO Box 143
Leicester LE1 9BH

Offers: BA (Hons) in Three-dimensional Design; MA in Interior Design

London College of Furniture
41 Commercial Road
London E1 1LA

Offers: B/TEC National Diploma in Design; B/TEC Higher National Diploma in Design

Manchester Polytechnic
Grosvenor Building, Cavendish Street
Manchester M15 6BR

Offers: BA (Hons) in Three-dimensional Design; MA in Interior Design

Middlesex Polytechnic
Cat Hill, Barnet
Hertfordshire EN4 8HT

Offers: BA (Hons) in Interior Design; MA in Interior Design

Newcastle upon Tyne College of Art and Technology
Rye Hill
Newcastle upon Tyne NE4 7SA

Offers: B/TEC Higher National Diploma in Spatial Design

Polytechnic of North London
Holloway Road
London N7 8DB

Offers: BA (Hons) in Interior Design

Portsmouth College of Art, Design and Further Education
Winston Churchill Avenue
Portsmouth PO1 2DJ

Offers: B/TEC National Diploma in Design

South Devon College of Arts and Technology
Newton Road
Torquay TQ2 5BY

Offers: B/TEC National Diploma in Interior and Three-dimensional Design

South Glamorgan Institute of Higher Education
Howard Gardens
Cardiff CF2 1SP

Offers: BA (Hons) in Interior Design

Trent Polytechnic
Dryden Street
Nottingham NG1 4FX

Offers: BA (Hons) in Interior Design

Worcester Technical College
Deansway
Worcester WR1 2JF

Offers: B/TEC National Diploma in Design

US Courses

Academy of Art College
2300 Stockton Street, San Francisco
California 94133

Offers: Bachelor of Interior Design

Alexandria Area Technical Institute
1600 Jefferson Street, Alexandria
Minnesota 56308

Offers: Associate of Interior Design

California State University
1250 Bellflower Boulevard
Long Beach, California 90840

Offers: Bachelor of Fine Arts in Interior Design

Chamberlayne Junior College
240 Newbury Street, Boston
Massachusetts 02116

Offers: Professional Certificate in Interior Design

Drexel University
33rd and Market Streets,
Philadelphia, Pennsylvania 19104

Offers: Bachelor of Science Interior Design Program

El Centro College
Main at Lamar, Dallas
Texas 75202

Offers: Certificate of Interior Design

Fashion Institute of Technology
227 West 27th Street, New York
NY 10001

Offers: Associate of Applied Science in Interior Design

Louisiana State University
Baton Rouge
Louisiana 70803

Offers: Bachelor of Interior Design

Mount Vernon College
2100 Foxhall Road North West
Washington DC 20007

Offers: Bachelor of Arts in Interior Design

New York School of Interior Design
155 East 56th Street, New York
NY 10022

Offers: Bachelor of Fine Arts Interior Design Program; Diploma in Interior Design

Canadian courses

Algonquin College
1385 Woodroffe, Nepean
Ontario K2G 1VA

Offers: Credit Programme in Interior Design

Dawson College
350 Selby Street, Montreal
Quebec H32 1W7

Offers: Credit Programme in Interior Design

Kwantlen College
9260-140 Street, Surrey
British Columbia V3T 5H8

Offers: Credit Programme in Interior Design

Mount Royal College
4825 Richard Road South West
Calgary, Alberta T3E 6K6

Offers: Credit Programme in Interior Design

University of Manitoba
Winnipeg
Manitoba R3T 2N2

Offers: Bachelor's Degree in Interior Design

Australian courses

Royal Melbourne Institute of Technology
GPO Box 2476V, Melbourne
Victoria 3001

Offers: BA (Interior Design); Graduate Diploma in Interior Design

South Australian College of Advanced Education
46 Kintore Avenue, Adelaide SA5000

Offers: Bachelor of Design

University of Technology, Sydney
PO Box 123
Broadway NSW2007

Offers: BA in Design; MA (Design); Graduate Diploma in Design Studies

New Zealand courses

The University of Auckland
Private Bag, Auckland

Offers: BFA Degree in Interior Design; MFA Degree in Interior Design

Glossary

Accents: small touches of a contrast colour.

Accent colour: a colour which adds emphasis by contrasting with the overall scheme.

Appliqué: a fabric motif, stitched on to cushions, wall-hangings etc. for decoration.

Base colour: the background colour used for a decorative paint technique, or mural.

Dado rails: carved wooden rails at waist level. Found in period houses.

Décor: decoration and furnishings

Drop: in wallpapering, the distance between ceiling and skirting board. In needlework, that between curtain rail and curtain hem.

Flat colour: in painting, a single colour of paint applied evenly over a surface.

Futon: Japanese sofabed consisting of a wooden bed-base and flexible mattress.

Hi-tech: short for high-technology. A streamlined style of decoration emphasizing the structure of things.

Mitre: in needlework or joinery, to join two pieces of fabric or wood at an angle of 45 degrees.

Motifs: decorative patterns or designs.

Pattern repeat: in wallpapering or needlework, the depth of one pattern. Used to calculate the amount of wastage in each drop when estimating quantities.

Perimeter: the outer boundary of a room or building.

Perspective: the technique of depicting a three-dimensional object on a flat surface.

Pinking shears: scissors with serrated blades, used for neatening fabric.

Plastic padding: pliable plastic substance for filling holes and blemishes in metal. Gives a tough, heat-resistant finish.

Primer: paint-like substance used to give an even, matt surface to areas to be painted. Usually coloured grey.

Ruches: in needlework, gathers in fabric which give it a puckered surface.

Selvedge: the firm edge of a piece of woven material, which prevents it from fraying.

Sheeting: fabric which is wide enough to make seamless sheets.

Slipstitch: a small, fairly weak stitch used for neatening and hemming.

Sugar soap: abrasive soap, used for cleaning walls and woodwork, prior to painting.

Template: a guide or pattern which can be drawn around to produce a regular shape. Usually made from card, metal or plastic.

Tie-backs: strips of fabric, cords or ribbons for tying curtains back during the daytime.

Tone: a value, or grade of colour

Top coat: in painting, the uppermost layer of paint.

Undercoat: in painting, a preparatory layer of paint. Usually applied between primer and top coat.

Veneered: a surface with a fine layer of good quality wood or plastic, usually concealing material of poorer quality.

Acknowledgements

The following companies and individuals generously gave advice, expertise and photographic facilities: Helen Giles Ltd (Interior Designers); Susan Giles; Butcher plastering specialists; Miller & Davies (Upholders) Ltd; Pullingers interiors and furnishing.

Fabric designs courtesy of: cover Collier Campbell Ltd, Warner Fabrics plc; title page and page 19 Collier Campbell Ltd, Warner Fabrics plc, Textra, John Lewis plc; page 2 Osborne & Little plc; pages 8-9 Designers Guild; page 22 Zoffany Ltd; pages 36-37 Collier Campbell Ltd; page 45 Osborne & Little plc.

Photographic credits

Front cover Crown Paints; page 2 Dulux; page 4 top Osborne & Little plc, centre and bottom EWA/A; pages 14-15 Camera Press; page 16 Camera Press; page 17 left Camera Press, centre Collier Campbell Ltd, right Camera Press; page 18 Camera Press; page 20 top Crown Paints, bottom left and right Dulux; page 22 Designers Guild; page 25 left EWA/A, centre Osborne & Little plc, right EWA/A; page 26 Crown Paints; page 28 top Crown Paints, centre la Maison de Marie Claire/Eriaud/Comte, bottom EWA/A; page 30 EWA/A; page 32 Camera Press; page 33 EWA/A, page 34 left Dulux, right Textra; page 36 Collier Campbell Ltd; page 39 EWA/A; page 43 left and centre Dulux, right Crown Paints; page 44 top and centre Camera Press; bottom Dulux; pages 46-47 Keith Parry.